heroine (think Katniss on a magic horse).'
Books, Bonnets and Full-Frontal Blogging

'This series should bring the Arthurian legends alive

for a new audience.' *The Bookseller*

LANCE OF TRUTH

PENDRAGON LEGACY

BOOK 2

LANCE OF TRUTH

KATHERINE ROBERTS

templar

A TEMPLAR BOOK

First published in the UK in 2012 by Templar Publishing,
This paperback edition published in 2013 by Templar
Publishing, an imprint of The Templar Company Limited,
Deepdene Lodge, Deepdene Avenue,
Dorking, Surrey, RH5 4AT, UK
www.templarco.co.uk

Copyright © 2012 by Katherine Roberts
Cover illustration by Scott Altmann

First paperback edition
1 3 5 7 9 10 8 6 4 2

ISBN 978-1-84877-866-5

Printed and bound by CPI Group (UK) Ltd, Croydon, CR0 4YY

JF

For my mother

For my mother

Contents

Characters

ALBA – Rhianna's mist horse, a white mare
   from Avalon.

ARIANRHOD – Rhianna's maid, ex-maid of
   Morgan Le Fay. Her cheek bears a scar
   in the shape of a pentacle.

CAI – young squire at Camelot who becomes
   Rhianna's champion.

CHIEF CYNRIC – leader of the Saxons.

ELPHIN – Prince of Avalon and only son of
   Lord Avallach.

EVENSTAR – Elphin's mist horse, a white
   stallion from Avalon.

GARETH – older squire, Cai's rival.

KING ARTHUR – king of Britain. His ghost
appears to Rhianna while his body
sleeps in Avalon awaiting rebirth.

LADY ISABEL – lady in charge of the damsels
at Camelot.

LORD AVALLACH – Lord of Avalon and
Elphin's father. Leader of the Wild Hunt.

MERLIN – King Arthur's druid. Morgan Le
Fay drowned his man's body but his
spirit lives in the body of a merlin
falcon. He can still work magic.

MORDRED – Rhianna's cousin and rival for
the throne; the son of Morgan Le Fay.

MORGAN LE FAY – King Arthur's sister and
Mordred's mother, a witch. Now dead,
her spirit advises Mordred from Annwn.

NIMUE – the Lady of the Lake, who took
King Arthur's sword Excalibur after

Arthur's death and gave it to Rhianna.

QUEEN GUINEVERE – Rhianna's mother, held
    prisoner by Mordred.

RHIANNA PENDRAGON – daughter of King
    Arthur, raised in Avalon.

SANDY – Cai's pony, rescued from the Saxons.

SIR AGRAVAINE – grumpy older knight.

SIR BEDIVERE – a young knight, also known as
    'Soft Hands' because of his gentle nature.

SIR BORS – leader of King Arthur's knights.

SIR LANCELOT – Arthur's champion knight,
    whose love for Queen Guinevere caused
    him to break the Lance of Truth when
    he fought against his king.

THE SHADRAKE – a dragon from Annwn,
    breathes ice instead of fire and hunts
    between worlds.

To Dragon Land

Druid
Beacon

SUMMER SEA

Lonely Tor
[Glastonbury]

Marshes

Stone
Circle

To Mines of
Lyonesse

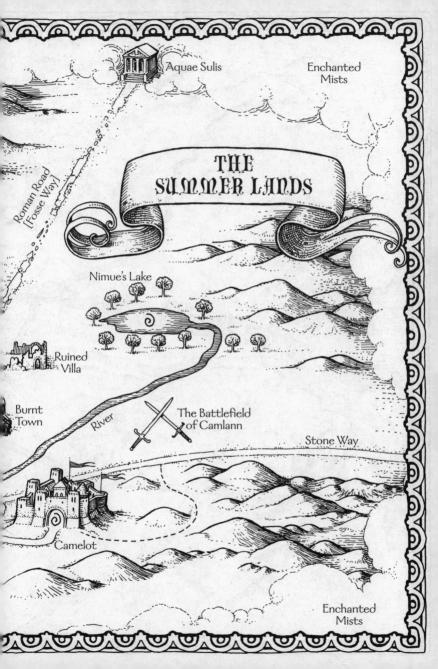

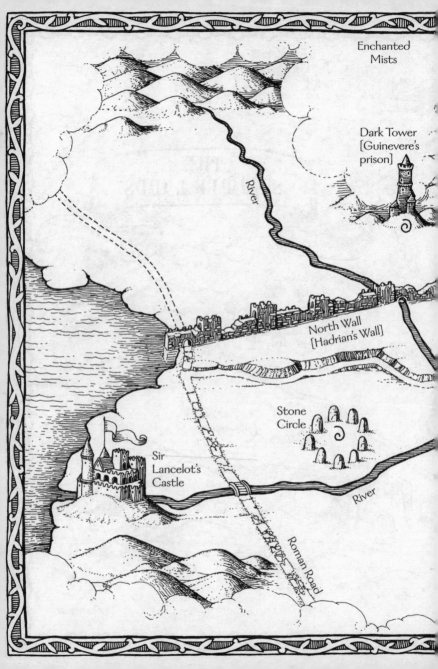

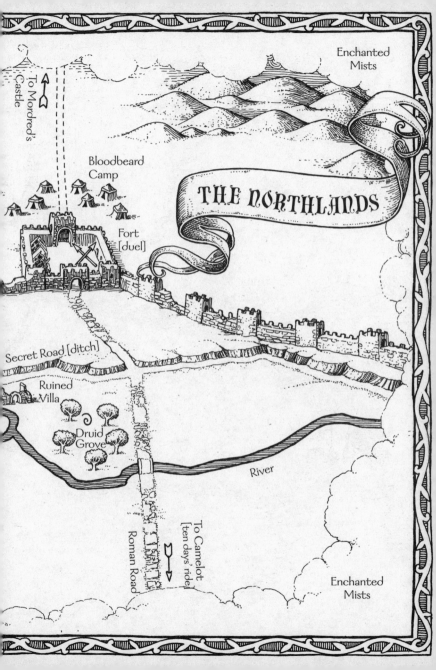

Enchanted Mists

To Mordred's Castle

Bloodbeard Camp

THE NORTHLANDS

Fort [duel]

Secret Road [ditch]

Ruined Villa

Druid Grove

River

To Camelot [ten days' ride]

Roman Road

Enchanted Mists

Four Lights stand against the dark:
The Sword Excalibur that was
forged in Avalon,
The Lance of Truth made by the
hands of men,
The Crown of Dreams, which hides
the jewel of Annwn,
And the Grail said to hold all the
stars in heaven.

THE DARK KNIGHT
SETS A TRAP

Mordred cast a final look around the cave where he'd spent the winter. Damp oozed from the rocky walls. His bed, where he had spent so much time suffering in the dark, would bear his bloodstains for ever.

He spat on it. "They will pay for my pain," he promised the shadows. "They will all pay."

He'd almost died of the wounds he had received last summer in the battle against his uncle, Arthur Pendragon. But now he felt stronger than before, in spite of his crippled leg and missing sword hand. King Arthur was dead, and Queen Guinevere his prisoner. His horse waited outside with his men. It would only be a matter of time until he dealt with Arthur's daughter, the girl who stood between him and the throne.

Before he left this place, he had one more thing to do. He pulled on a black gauntlet with his teeth. Then he picked up the mirror his mother had given him so he could spy on the world of men. The cracked glass glittered as Mordred breathed on it.

He saw the tower that served as his Aunt Guinevere's prison. It was more comfortable than his own sanctuary, but the queen seemed not to appreciate it. She had tried to escape, and he'd been forced to send his bloodbeards to chain her to the bed. But she didn't know why she was a captive yet. He'd been looking forward to this moment all winter.

He lit candles so she would be able to see him properly and put on his silver torque. He waited until she was combing her filthy hair and whispered, "Aunt Guinevere."

She jumped. The chain on her wrist clanked as her comb stilled. "Mordred," she whispered. "You can't keep me here for ever! Lancelot will find me. Then he'll hunt you down and send your dark soul to join your mother's in Annwn for all eternity."

Mordred smiled, bored with her empty threats. He'd already made plans to take care of her champion. "Your precious Lancelot won't need to hunt me down. Unlike him, I'm not a coward to run away from my fights. I've issued him a challenge. A joust to the death with you as the prize. You'll enjoy watching, I think."

She gripped the comb tightly, a flicker of hope in her eyes. "Lancelot carries the Lance of Truth! No knight has ever bested him in a duel. He'll kill you."

Mordred chuckled. "Oh, I doubt it. The lance is broken, as you well know. Without it, Lancelot's no greater than an ordinary knight. Whereas *I* will be fighting with the Sword of Light."

The queen went still. "Excalibur was returned to Nimue's lake," she said uncertainly. "The Lady of the Lake would never let a witch's brat like you have it!"

"No need to be rude," Mordred told her. "You really are behind with the news, aren't you? I suppose you've been a bit out of touch this winter, so I'll update you. My cousin Rhianna has got the sword back from Nimue, and will shortly be bringing it to me. You look puzzled, Aunt. Surely you remember your sweet baby daughter, with the cute freckled nose, the one you abandoned to the fairies? She's grown quite a bit since you last saw her. She's been in the world of men for some time now, looking for you. Maybe I'll let her keep you company in your tower. I wonder if you'll dare call me a witch's brat then?"

The comb clattered to the floor. The queen backed against the wall as far as the chain would allow and wrapped her arms around her body. "Oh God…" she whispered. "Rhianna… where is she? If you dare lay a hand on her—"

"Oh, I've already laid a hand on her,"

Mordred said, lifting his severed wrist and grimacing at the memory of using the shadow magic. "She knows my power. Just not my plans for her – yet. We had a little, um, *misunderstanding* the last time we spoke, so I can't use the Round Table to send my message. But she should be receiving it any day now. Sometimes the old ways can be more persuasive, don't you think?"

The queen blinked and shook her head. "She won't bring you Excalibur! My daughter wouldn't be that stupid."

Mordred smiled again. "Ah, but you don't know her as well as I do. Believe me, she can be remarkably stupid once she gets a sword in her hand."

◀️ 1 ▶️

Joust

At Camelot they joust in spring
To test the knights who serve the king
When a damsel down the course did ride
Enchantments round her for disguise.

The first joust to be held at Camelot since King Arthur's death drew a big crowd. Word had spread during the winter that Arthur's daughter had made a peace treaty with the Saxons, and everyone wanted to catch a glimpse of the brave young princess who was rumoured to carry her father's magic sword, Excalibur, and to have fought a dragon with it – though few people actually believed that part of the story, of course. A damsel fight a dragon? That didn't even happen in songs.

Unaware of what they were saying about her, Rhianna leaned out of her window to watch the steady stream of people coming up the hill. The breeze blew her unruly copper hair across her eyes. She brushed it away impatiently. She'd hoped her mother would be back by now. But there was still no sign of the queen or the champion knight Sir Lancelot, who had taken her north last winter to keep her safe from the fighting. Soon the knights would ride in search of her, and Rhianna did not plan on being left behind.

She turned her attention to the area outside

the walls, where the squires' tilt would take place later that day. When all the boys had ridden, the winner would be allowed to try his skill against a grown knight. The squires would not carry full-length lances. Instead, they would use light spears with blunted ends that shattered easily. Rhianna reckoned she could handle one, no problem. But when she had asked Sir Bors if she could enter the tilt on her mist horse Alba, he'd just laughed.

"Nobody'll dare tilt against the Pendragon's daughter!" he'd said. "Your father never entered a joust himself after he became king. He let his champion knight tilt for him. No, Damsel Rhianna, let the squires have their fun. Besides, it's just as much fun watchin' them, believe me."

Rhianna never liked watching when she could be doing. But she supposed it would be embarrassing to have Alba mist under her and to fall off in front of everyone. She had her own plans for today, and they did not include playing the princess so everyone could gape at her. She'd had quite enough of that over the winter.

A knock at the door broke into her thoughts.

"My lady?" Her maid Arianrhod hurried in, breathless from the stairs, her arms full of green material with a gold circlet resting on top. "It's a beautiful morning! Everyone's really excited to see you! You should get dressed now."

"I am dressed," Rhianna said. "Almost, anyway."

She was already wearing the tunic and leggings she used for riding. She quickly opened her clothing chest and slipped her Avalonian armour over the top. The silvery moons glimmered in the early light. She fingered them thoughtfully, remembering how they had stopped an arrow last year when Mordred's bloodbeards had captured her. She hadn't been able to test the armour against a lance. She just hoped the magic would work in the same way.

Arianrhod laid the dress and jewels on the bed. She eyed the armour. "Are you worried Mordred might try something?" she asked sympathetically. "Because you needn't be. Security's always tight for a joust, so you won't need that under your dress today. It'll be warm when the sun gets up. You'll get sweaty, I'm warning you."

"I'll get sweaty all right." Rhianna grinned as she strapped Excalibur's red scabbard around her waist.

She rested her hand on the white jewel set

into the hilt of the sword. A brightness filled her. *The strength of a hundred men.* Well, ninety-nine anyway, since she'd unknighted Mordred and banished his dark spirit from the magical jewel. She marched purposefully to the door.

"My lady... Rhia! You can't go out there before all those people looking like that!"

Arianrhod's horrified tone made her hesitate. She didn't want to get her friend into trouble.

"I can't wear a dress today," she explained gently. "They've come to see Excalibur, and a sword over a dress looks stupid. Besides, I don't want them to see me as a princess today. If they're going to believe we can hold Camelot against Mordred and his bloodbeards, they've got to see me as Rhianna *Pendragon*."

Arianrhod bit her lip. She picked up the

golden circlet and twisted it between her fingers. The pentacle-shaped scar on her cheek – a souvenir from her old mistress, Lady Morgan – pulsed crimson. "You haven't even brushed your hair," she said. "Some of those people have come a long way to see you."

Rhianna thought of the helm she'd borrowed from the armoury and hidden under the woodpile near the gates, and the mess it would make of her hair. But she wouldn't be wearing that until later.

She sat on the bed. "All right," she said. "You can braid my hair. But if anyone asks where I am when the squires' tilt finishes, I've gone riding with Elphin."

Her friend's fingers stilled. "You're not going to do anything stupid, are you?" she said.

"When do I ever do anything stupid?"

"All the time!"

Rhianna laughed as she reached for her father's battered shield with its red dragon design. "Don't worry about me. I'll be as careful as I usually am."

Arianrhod gave her a sideways look. She had got used to treating Rhianna's bruises after she came back from a training session with the squires. "I'll get the ointment ready," she said with a sigh.

❧

Rhianna found the Avalonian prince Elphin in the stables. He was helping Cai, the plump squire who had been with the knights when she and Elphin rode through the mists from Avalon, get his equally plump pony ready for the tilt. Elphin's extra fingers made short work of the buckles, which was just as well because Cai's seemed to be all thumbs. The noise was incredible. Horses neighed and trod on toes, while the squires yelled challenges at one another as they hurried to be first out on the course.

"Good luck, Cai!" she called.

The squire grimaced and patted the pony. "I'm going to need it, and so is Sandy."

"Who are you tilting against?"

He pulled a face. "Gareth. I reckon he fixed the draw."

"If he did, then he's braver than I thought," Elphin said, winking at Rhianna. "Good job you'll only be using wooden swords today."

Cai flushed.

Rhianna smiled. Even after a whole winter's training, a weapon in Cai's hand could be more dangerous to his friends than to his enemies.

"Don't worry, you'll be all right." Elphin picked up his harp, which he carried at all times in a deerskin bag, his eyes violet with amusement.

She wondered if he was planning to use magic to help their friend, because that was the only way she could see Cai winning a tilt against Gareth. She just hoped he would have some magic left over for her when she needed it.

A soft nose nudged her from over the stall. *It is very noisy in here this morning*, said Alba, the mare Lord Avallach had given her from the enchanted Avalonian herd. *Can we go galloping in the wood again? I promise I will not mist if you do not want me to.*

Rhianna smiled as she slipped into the mist horse's stable and quickly brushed her silver coat. "Not today, my darling. We're going to the meadow, where you can race as fast as you like."

That sounds fun, Alba said, with a pleased snort.

"It's going to be fun seeing everyone's faces afterwards," she said, leading the little mare out into the spring sunshine.

Sir Bedivere waited at the gates, handing out lances. The young knight did not seem surprised to see Rhianna dressed in her armour and riding Alba, though the other knights frowned at her.

"Who's going to answer the squires' challenge?" she asked him, hoping it wouldn't be the grumpy Sir Agravaine. She'd seen the dark-haired knight use his lance in battle, and didn't fancy being on the wrong end of it.

"I am," Sir Bedivere said, smiling at her. "Don't worry, I'll be gentle with whoever it is. Once they've eaten mud a couple of times, they usually lose their bravado pretty quick."

Rhianna relaxed slightly. "And what if he knocks you off?"

Sir Bedivere laughed. "Then I'll knight the lad myself! The others might call me 'Soft Hands', but no one except Lancelot's ever bested me in a fair tilt. Better clear the course, Damsel Rhianna. We're almost ready to start."

Hoping Elphin would remember to bring the helm from the woodpile, she trotted Alba over to the benches, where Arianrhod and the other damsels were already sitting in an excited group. The crowd had not noticed her yet, but it would only be a matter of time. Over in the horse lines the knights rushed about, tightening girths and giving their squires last-moment instructions.

A horn blew, and Sir Bors mounted the steps to announce the start of the spring joust.

He made a gruff speech about Sir Lancelot and Queen Guinevere being on their way back to hold Camelot for King Arthur's return, and Excalibur keeping their lands safe in the meantime. He wasn't a very good speaker, and the crowd got restless. They peered at the stands, obviously trying to spot Rhianna. Someone pointed at Lady Isabel, who looked after the Damsel Tower.

"There she is…!"

"Are you sure? She's older than I thought."

"No, that's the woman in charge of the damsels, silly… what about that dark girl? She's about the right age."

Arianrhod ducked her head, though not quickly enough to hide her cheek.

"Ugh!" a woman said. "Where'd she get that horrid scar? In Avalon?"

Rhianna saw Elphin in the stands with his harp cradled in his lap. Its bag, under the bench between his feet, bulged strangely. He patted it, and she smiled.

"Damsel Rhianna, you'd better show them Excalibur now," Sir Bedivere whispered.

She realised Sir Bors had stopped talking and people were staring around expectantly. She trotted Alba out on the course and drew her sword. The blade flashed in the sun.

A hush fell over the crowd as Excalibur's jewel brightened, haloing her and Alba in silver light. She thought she saw her father's ghost in the stands, smiling at her, and new energy and confidence filled her.

"As you can see, Princess Rhianna carries the Sword of Light that was forged in Avalon!" Sir Bors announced. "She'll keep Camelot and our lands safe from the barbarians till King Arthur is well enough to return from Avalon and sit on the throne again."

A few people whispered uneasily. "And what if King Arthur doesn't come back?" someone called. "You expect us to believe a damsel can handle Excalibur? It needs a man's hand."

Another man said loudly, "Why's the girl wearing armour? No prince is going to want to marry her looking like that!" His companions quickly shushed him. But others in the crowd were muttering now, confused.

Rhianna sighed. She had become used to this.

She raised her voice, which carried easily across the field. "I am Rhianna Pendragon! I'm wearing armour because it was a gift from Lord Avallach of Avalon, and I carry King

Arthur's shield, which Merlin gave to me when he brought my father's body through the mists. This is my father's sword, Excalibur, given to me by Lady Nimue of the Lake last year so we could defeat the Saxons, and I can handle it just fine."

She made Alba prance slowly along the barrier and trot back down the other side, showing the doubters her sword. As she did so, she measured the distance and checked the ground. When she reached the stands again, she sliced Excalibur through the air in a pattern of sparkling light, sketching a dragon.

Sir Bors scowled at her for showing off. But it worked. The horns blew again, and the crowd cheered as another fanfare announced the start of the joust.

Sir Bors had been right. It was quite funny, watching the squires tilt. Most lost their nerve at the last moment and missed each other's shields completely, to the sound of whistles and boos from the stands. A couple of boys fell off as their ponies started down the course, making people laugh. Those who did manage to score a hit usually dropped their spears or galloped out of control across the meadow afterwards. But apart from a few bruises, nobody got hurt.

Gareth and Cai were the last pair to tilt.

Rhianna sat up straighter in her saddle. "Watch carefully, because we're next," she whispered to Alba.

The mare pricked her white ears and snorted. *Stupid sort of race. They gallop in opposite directions.*

The horn sounded, and the two ponies broke

into a gallop. Sandy clearly enjoyed jousting, and Cai nearly fell off over his tail as the plump horse leaped forwards. Gareth's pony was slower to start, but the older boy had his spear lowered first. He aimed the point at the squire's shield with a determined expression. Cai looked terrified.

Rhianna winced as the two ponies came together. She fingered Excalibur's hilt, wondering if she could use the blade to flash sunlight into Gareth's eyes, as she had done to confuse the dragon in the battle last year. But it seemed a bit silly to use the Sword of Light for such a trick. As Cai galloped closer, Elphin reached for his harp.

No wonder his pony runs away with him, Alba said. *He is not looking where he is going.*

Rhianna grinned, and almost missed the quick flicker of her friend's fingers across his harp strings. As the two boys met, the air around them sparkled. Gareth's spear seemed to slide off Cai's shield. At the same time, Cai's spear slipped past Gareth's shield and struck him squarely on the chest. The older squire fell off over his pony's tail with a grunt of surprise. Arianrhod leaped to her feet with a cheer. Gareth's friends groaned.

Sir Bedivere trotted his chestnut stallion to the end of the barrier. Someone passed him a light squire's spear, which he fooled around with to make the crowd laugh. While the knights were distracted, catching the loose pony and organising the other squires to rake the course for the challenge, Rhianna eased her borrowed helm out of Elphin's bag.

Her friend's eyes turned violet. "You're not still going through with this?"

"Of course," Rhianna said, twisting her hair up under the helm and pulling down the face guard. "I have to show the knights I can look after myself in a fight, or they won't let me ride north with them to look for my mother and the Lance of Truth."

"Be careful, Rhia. I'm not sure Father's smith made that armour to withstand a lance."

"I've been training all winter! I'm not going to let Sir Bedivere spear me, don't worry. Just play your harp so they don't recognise me until it's too late."

Before anyone could stop her, she had snatched the spear from Cai's hand, exchanged her Pendragon shield for his plain one, and trotted her little mist horse to the far end of the barrier.

Sir Agravaine squinted at her as she lined up.

"We have a brave squire to take up the challenge!" he announced. The crowd – in the mood now for a good laugh – cheered. "Sir Bedivere tilts against Squire, er…?"

Even as the old knight's eyes narrowed in suspicion, Elphin's harp tinkled from the stands. The air around Rhianna sparkled, just like it had when Cai knocked Gareth out of his saddle. Alba's mane shimmered. Sir Agravaine's face went blank. He lifted the horn to his lips and blew.

Excitement shivered through her as Sir Bedivere's chestnut horse leaped forward. Rhianna crouched low over her mare's neck, tucked the spear under her armpit, and grinned as Alba sprang eagerly into a gallop to meet him. She couldn't see much through the helm, which had a narrow slit to protect the eyes from splinters, but she did her best to aim at the centre of the knight's shield.

The noise of the crowd surged around her like the sea. The Avalonian music filled her head. She felt dizzy. *Just don't let him recognise me*, she willed. *I only need one chance.*

Sir Bedivere obviously couldn't see very much either. His lance stayed low as the distance between them closed. Rhianna set her jaw, kept her shield steady and refused to think about what would happen if she missed. She had to strike first. If he knocked her off, the knights would never let her ride north with them.

As she braced herself for the crash, she heard large hoof beats behind her. The crowd gasped. Sir Bedivere squinted through his helm in alarm, and his lance jerked up.

Rhianna's heart sank. The knights must have recognised Alba. Elphin's magic must not be strong enough to hide a mist horse. So now they were going to embarrass her by dragging her off the field in front of everyone.

She thought about taking advantage of Sir Bedivere's hesitation to get past his guard. But she couldn't bring herself to do it. At the last moment, she jerked her spear up, too. The ribbon tied to the end slapped Sir Bedivere across the eyes as they galloped past each other, and the crowd groaned.

Looking over her shoulder, she saw a big black horse. She wondered which knight had come after her. Whoever it was couldn't ride very well. He was jerking at the reins, flopping back and forth over his horse's neck. People scattered from its path, screaming.

Alba flattened her ears. *Is it another race?*

Rhianna thought of everyone watching the black horse chase her and Alba across the river, and sighed. Even more embarrassing. "No." She slowed the mare and tugged off her helm, ready to fight with words rather than a spear.

But the black horse didn't stop when she did. Foaming with sweat, it charged on past, so close that Alba misted in alarm. Rhianna grabbed the mare's mane and drew Excalibur. Its rider jerked backwards again as the horse passed them, and she saw why. The knight had been roped into his saddle with the reins tied around his wrists. His throat had been cut.

Alba whinnied, and the runaway horse slowed to a trot. It turned and came back, carrying its grisly burden. The two horses held a short conversation, snorting into each other's nostrils.

He says a dragon chased him, the mare reported. *He has galloped for many days. His legs are very tired. Bad men kill his rider.*

Rhianna kept hold of Excalibur, wary. She'd seen too many of Mordred's tricks to trust a dead knight. A slave collar had been buckled around his neck, stiff with blood and strangely marked.

By this time, Sir Bors and Sir Agravaine and several of the squires on their ponies had caught up. She saw Elphin running across the field with his harp, with Arianrhod and Cai close behind.

"Stay away from him, Damsel Rhianna!" Sir Bors warned, pushing between Alba and the black horse.

Sir Agravaine warily lifted the rider's head and peered into his face. "One of Sir Lancelot's men," he grunted. "What's that written around his neck?"

Sir Bors used his sword to cut the collar from the dead man. He turned it over, examining the marks on it. He frowned. "It's in the old druid language. We'll need to get the priest to translate. But I recognise that signature…" He looked at them grimly. "It's signed Mordred Pendragon, Emperor of Britain."

2

A Message
from Mordred

By dead man's hand the message came
Bearing rules for Mordred's game.
A druid sees what the dark words mean:
Arthur's sword for the life of a queen.

With all the excitement caused by the runaway horse, people soon forgot about Rhianna's embarrassing tilt. Some of the crowd even seemed to think it had been part of the show, and cheered her as she rode back across the field with her bodyguard of wary knights. A few people – those close enough to see the dead man's blood-soaked collar – crossed themselves and muttered about witchcraft. The rest headed for the food stalls in search of lunch.

The knights remained grim. Back inside Camelot, Sir Bors ordered the gates barred and called a meeting of the Round Table for that afternoon. He scowled at Rhianna. "You'd better bring Excalibur so we can try to contact Lancelot using the spirit channel. But you can count yourself lucky you're a damsel. If you were a boy, I'd order you whipped! What you did out there was very stupid. What if poor Bedivere had killed you?"

Rhianna lifted her chin. "He wouldn't have killed me. Alba and I have been practising."

"Jousting against trees?" Sir Bors grunted. "Oh yes, Damsel Rhianna. I'm not blind. And seems to me you've been fallin' off quite a bit, judging by all the mud on your backside when you come back from the woods with your fairy friend! The jousting field's no place for a damsel. It's how we learn to kill each other. You want to end up like this poor chap of Lancelot's?"

Rhianna flushed. She looked at the dead man, worried. If Mordred had killed Lancelot's man, what had happened to Sir Lancelot and her mother?

"Ought've let Bedivere teach the girl a lesson," Sir Agravaine growled, ordering the squires to untie the dead knight and take his exhausted horse to the stables. "Might have knocked some sense into her."

She eyed Sir Bedivere, braced for his anger, too.

But as they led their horses to the stables, the young knight whispered, "Cheer up, Damsel Rhianna. It was my fault as much as yours. I recognised you halfway down the course. Thought I'd scare you into pulling up, but I should have known better. King Arthur's daughter doesn't scare that easily! Good job Mordred's message arrived when it did, though – for a nasty moment back there, I thought you were going to knock *me* off in front of everyone. I'd never have lived it down."

In spite of her worry, Rhianna managed a smile. "I'm sorry, Sir Bedivere," she said. "I didn't mean to get you into trouble. I just wanted to prove I can look after myself in a fight so Sir Bors will let me ride north with you, and now..." Her voice broke.

The knight patted her arm. "I know you're worried about your mother," he said gently. "But we'll find out what's happened to her, never fear. You see to your mare and have something to eat. We'll all think better on full stomachs."

⚜

The last thing Rhianna felt like doing was eating. She couldn't stop thinking about that blood-soaked collar and its grisly message. What if the priest translated it wrongly? She needed to talk to Merlin. As soon as she'd settled Alba, she hurried through the tunnel to the hawk mews.

A small, grey-blue falcon dozed on a perch

in the shadows. She plucked off its hood. It blinked a pale blue eye at her then stuck its head grumpily under its wing.

"Merlin?" she whispered, prodding it.

Her father's druid had been ambushed by Morgan Le Fay as he brought them through the mists from Avalon last year, leaving his spirit roaming the world of men in search of another body. He'd chosen his namesake, the merlin falcon, after failing to control the dragon he'd tried to inhabit first of all. Sometimes she wished he'd stayed in the dragon.

"Merlin!" she hissed. "I know you can hear me. This is important."

The little bird opened its beak and screeched at her.

She quickly put her hand on Excalibur's jewel. As the magic of her sword lit up the drifting feathers, the screech turned into words.

"—been up to, child, and I don't want to know. But I thought you'd be back when you needed me. I gather Mordred's causing trouble again? If you'd kept me in your room, like I suggested in the first place, this mightn't have happened."

"I told you, feathers make me sneeze. Why can't you find another body? Something more useful like a dog or a horse?"

Merlin laughed. "Dogs and horses can't fly. Being a hawk is more fun than I thought it would be. Hunting's good around this place, plenty of fat mice. I always told Arthur he ought to do something about them before they ate all of Camelot's grain... stop scowling, Rhianna Pendragon! It makes you look like a barbarian. So tell me what's happened.

You obviously haven't just come in here for a chat, all splattered in mud like you are."

Rhianna frowned. "One of Sir Lancelot's men came with a message from Mordred," she said. "But he was dead when he got here, and Sir Bors says it's in druid language so we don't know what it says yet."

"Ah yes, the secret ogham alphabet. The Romans never did manage to break our code. Good to see Prince Mordred remembers his lessons." Merlin hopped to the end of his perch and cocked his head. "Well, where is it then?"

"What?"

"The message, girl! Have you grown stupid as well as foolhardy over the winter?"

Rhianna scowled again. "Sir Bors took it. It's scratched on a slave collar... covered in blood." She shuddered at the memory.

The merlin blinked. "Whose blood?"

"The dead knight's, I suppose…"

"Never *suppose*," Merlin said. "Things are not always what they seem, especially where witchcraft is concerned."

Rhianna's stomach fluttered. "You don't think it was my moth—"

"No, child. If Mordred's got hold of your mother, which I have to say is a distinct possibility by the sounds of things, the last thing he'll do is hurt her. She's far too valuable as a hostage." He cocked his head and fixed her with a pale eye. "This message will be Mordred's terms for her release. You must be prepared for that. Don't let your emotions rule your head."

"But what if—" She bit her lip, not wanting to voice her fears.

Merlin was pacing up and down his perch,

wings spread for balance. "Let me think. I need to get a look at that message. Don't expect the knights know what's happened to me yet? Good, then we just need an excuse to get me into the meeting. Best thing would be to let me loose in the courtyard. Then I can fly in through the hole in the roof above the Round Table, and you can say you're training me to come to your wrist. We just need to make sure they hear me before they throw me out."

"How?" Rhianna said. "I can't hear you unless I'm touching Excalibur. Do you mean I have to give them my sword?" She tightened her hand possessively on the hilt.

"Of course not! The Round Table has magic of its own. In King Arthur's day it would have been easy. But most of the knights are old men now, hardened in their ways and deaf to the spirit world, so we'll have to choose carefully. The ones who might have been some use to us died on the Grail Quest. Young Bedivere's about the most open-minded of those who are left. Old Bors tries his best, but Agravaine would sooner fight than talk. They never much liked the idea of me taking King Arthur's body to Avalon—" His words ended in another screech.

He had been talking so much, he'd missed the end of the perch. He hung upside-down from the jesses that tethered him in the mews, beating his wings. He looked so funny, Rhianna forgot her worry over Mordred's message and giggled.

"Are you laughing at me, Rhianna Pendragon?" Merlin regained his balance and fluffed his feathers indignantly. "Better hurry up and free me. We've got company."

Rhianna drew Excalibur and whirled to see

Arianrhod standing nervously at the door.

"My lady!" the girl gasped, staring at her blade. "This is Camelot. You don't need to draw your sword in here."

Rhianna frowned at her friend and slid Excalibur back into its red scabbard. "You shouldn't creep up on people like that. What do you want?"

"I came to tell you the knights have been in the Great Hall yelling at each other since they got back from the field. Aren't you supposed to be at the meeting? They sent me to find you, but no one knew where you were. Then Elphin said you might be in here talking to your hawk. Don't you think finding out what's happened to the queen is a bit more important?"

"What do you think I'm trying to do?"

Rhianna tugged the jesses free of the perch

and hurried out into the courtyard with the merlin flapping on her wrist. His talons drew blood, but she hardly felt the pain. She released the bird and dashed back into the castle. Ignoring Arianrhod's pleas for her to bathe first, she ran down the long corridors, her fists clenched in anger. They'd started without her again!

She pushed past the guards and barged through the double doors into the Great Hall. She'd grown strong with all her sword training and riding over the winter. The heavy doors crashed back against the wall with a satisfying clang.

The knights with their backs to the door twisted round in alarm, hands groping for sword hilts that were not there. Nobody was allowed to sit at the Round Table armed, except the Pendragon.

"Ah, Rhianna," Sir Bors said, giving her a sympathetic smile. "There you are. Come and sit down." He patted the chair next to him.

Rhianna narrowed her eyes at him, suspicious. Why was he being so nice to her?

She felt a bit self-conscious as the knights watched her walk round to the empty seat, where Sir Bors had already hung her father's shield with the red dragon prancing across it. Seeing it there, she remembered that she'd left it on the jousting field this morning and felt bad about that.

Then she saw the blood-soaked slave collar on the table and forgot everything else.

She sat, and the guards – after a questioning look at Sir Bors – closed the doors again to seal the hall.

Sir Agravaine cleared his throat. "Er,

Rhianna," he said. "We asked the priest to help us out with the ogham..."

"Druid language," Sir Bedivere explained.

"I know what the ogham is," Rhianna said impatiently, making the knight raise an eyebrow. "What does it say?"

Sir Agravaine went on, "As far as we can make out, it says Mordred has kidnapped the queen, and he's demanding we take him Excalibur in exchange for her life. Of course there's no question of letting Mordred keep your father's sword. But we've decided that, under the circumstances, we'd best take Excalibur to him so we can get Guinevere somewhere safe. Then, once we've found out what's happened to Lancelot, maybe we can think about getting the sword back—"

"No!" Rhianna leaped to her feet. "We can't

give Mordred the Sword of Light! I need it to find the other three Lights to heal my father, you know that."

Without Excalibur, she didn't see how she was going to succeed in her quest, especially not if Mordred had taken the Lance of Truth from Sir Lancelot... though that was meant to be broken, so maybe it didn't matter?

The knights frowned at her. "The queen must be our first concern," Sir Bors said. "Arthur's dead and awaiting rebirth in Avalon. There's not much we can do about that. Your mother's alive. Let's keep it that way."

She couldn't think straight. "But I thought we were going to try contacting Lancelot using the spirit magic?" she said, her stomach doing strange things. "Surely he'll answer if my mother's in danger?" She rested her hand on

Excalibur's hilt, daring them to stop her from trying the magic.

The knights glanced at one another.

Sir Bedivere put his hand over hers. "No, Rhianna," he said. "We've changed our minds. If Mordred's got hold of Lancelot as well, and we use the spirit magic to summon him, we'll be as good as inviting the dark knight in here. We can't risk it."

She closed her eyes, trying to think. What had Sir Agravaine said? Mordred wanted the Sword of Light in exchange for her mother's life… If he did have the Lance, that would give her cousin two of the Lights. Which was more important, her mother or her quest?

Her hand trembled on her sword hilt. Sir Bedivere slipped an arm around her shoulders and gave her a little squeeze. "Don't worry,

Damsel Rhianna," he said. "It might not be necessary to actually give the sword to Mordred. We'll work it out, you'll see."

Rhianna shrugged him off, her head spinning. "Where's Elphin? He should be here. He'll help us if Mordred tries any dark magic. He did before."

The knights muttered uneasily. Sir Bors sighed, and said, "We've decided it's best to keep the contents of this message to ourselves. The Avalonian boy might pass it back to his father, and who knows what the fairy lord might do to stop us takin' the Sword of Light to Mordred. Cai told us what happened at midwinter."

Rhianna frowned. The last time Elphin had played his harp at a Round Table meeting, he'd stopped the magic so that they could not contact Merlin or anyone else. Then he'd led her into the snowy woods, where the Wild Hunt had surrounded them and tried to take Excalibur. Only the timely arrival of Cai and Arianrhod with the squires and damsels had stopped Lord Avallach from forcing her to give up the sword.

"Elphin won't try that again," she said. "He didn't understand. He thought he was protecting me."

"We can't risk it," Sir Bors insisted, shaking his head. "The fewer people who know, the better. We wouldn't have told you, except we're goin' to need to take Excalibur with us when we ride."

"But I'll be…" Rhianna looked at their faces. And then she knew. They meant to take Excalibur with them when they rode north to rescue her mother, and leave her behind in Camelot with the other damsels.

Not if she could help it!

She tightened her fist on Excalibur's white jewel and eyed the circle of sky above the Round Table. A cloud crossed the sun, plunging the hall into shadow. "Hurry up, Merlin," she muttered, hoping he hadn't been distracted by a mouse.

"I'm sorry, Damsel Rhianna," Sir Bors began. "But we've already decided. Now sit down, and let's discuss this sensibly…"

Just then there was a flutter of wings, and the merlin spiralled down through the hole in the roof to land on the back of Sir Agravaine's chair. She watched the bird in relief, wondering whether to draw her sword to help the knights hear him.

As the men chuckled, distracted from their business, Merlin hopped on to Sir Agravaine's shoulder and peered at the collar. "Hmm, mmm… that fool Mordred never could spell to save his life… ah, I see… clever little devil. I smell Morgan Le Fay's hand in this…" He fluttered down on to the table and tried to turn the collar over to read the scratches on the other side, but his beak was not strong enough to lift the blood-soaked leather.

He spread his wings and muttered a spell. Nothing happened.

"Curse the witch," he grumbled. "I need my druid staff for this work."

Rhianna fought a smile as Sir Agravaine scowled at the little hawk and shooed it away. "Damn birds, making a mess everywhere. Is that your falcon, Damsel Rhianna? Get hold of it before it fouls the Round Table. This would never have happened in Arthur's day. If it's scratched the stone, we'll be in trouble."

He turned the collar over to check underneath. Merlin winked at Rhianna and immediately started reading the other side, avoiding Sir Agravaine's annoyed grabs at him.

"Hurry up, Merlin!" she hissed.

The knights frowned as the little hawk flew low over their heads. Sir Bors got to his feet with an irritated expression. "Damsel Rhianna, if you don't get hold of that bird right this moment, I'll—"

But she never found out what he'd do, because Sir Bors' eyes widened when the merlin landed on his head and whispered in his ear. Sir Bedivere was giving the bird a wary look. Merlin flew over to his chair and whispered to him, too. The young knight started.

"All right, Rhianna," the druid said. "You can use the sword in the table now. Carefully."

She hesitated. "Are you sure it's safe?"

"Want to see your mother, don't you? If these idiot knights are going to go tramping all the way up to the North Wall with Excalibur, it makes sense to know if the queen's actually in trouble first. Go on. Mordred can't hurt you while I'm here."

She kicked off her boots, stood on her chair and stepped barefoot on to the table. "Very well," she said to the knights, "if you won't let Elphin in here, then I'll just have to try the magic without him." She drew Excalibur in a hiss of silver sparks and held the shining blade over the sword-sized hole at the centre.

"No, Damsel Rhianna!" Sir Agravaine leaped to his feet.

She closed her eyes and lowered the sword. Energy fizzed up her arms. The knights scraped their chairs, and she heard mutters of anger.

Warily, she opened her eyes. The last time she'd opened the spirit channel in here with Excalibur, her cousin Mordred's shadow had sat in one of the chairs and told her King Arthur would not wake for thousands of years.

This time, her cousin did not appear. Instead, a ghostly lady occupied the seat Rhianna had just left. Hair the colour of dirty flames fell in tangles across her face. Freckles dusted her nose. Her eyes, though red-rimmed from crying, were a fierce green. Rhianna swallowed. It was like looking into a mirror and seeing an older version of herself, complete with dirt and bruises as if the ghost had just ridden in a joust, too. A long chain circled one wrist and stretched away into the shadows at the edge of the hall.

"Queen Guinevere!" Sir Bors cried, leaping to his feet. "Don't you worry, my lady, we're comin' to rescue you as soon as we can."

"Sir Bors… is that you? Is that the Round Table?" The queen stared around at the knights in confusion. "But Arthur's dead, so how…?" Then she looked up and saw Rhianna holding Excalibur. Her eyes widened. She reached out a ghostly arm, the chain clanking. *"Is that my Rhianna?"* she whispered. "Oh God, I thought Mordred was lying to me! You're meant to be safe in Avalon… It's true, then."

Rhianna discovered her throat had closed. She swallowed. "Mother?" she managed in the end. "Where are you?"

The queen took a deep breath. "I'm not sure. A tower on some godforsaken moor. It's always misty outside. There's some enchantment on it,

I think. Mordred says you'll never find it."

"We'll see about that," Sir Agravaine growled. "Where's that idiot Lancelot? Is he dead? Because if he's still alive and he let Mordred take you, I'll…"

The queen's gaze shifted, and she looked at something beside her that they could not see. She stiffened and shouted, "Don't come, Rhianna darling! It's a trick—"

Shadows rippled across her face, which blurred and shifted, making Rhianna dizzy. Excalibur twisted in her hands. Those knights who had sat down leaped to their feet again.

"Rhianna Pendragon!" Merlin's voice commanded. "Put that sword away. Now!"

With some relief, Rhianna returned the blade to its scabbard. The shadows and her mother's image vanished. She shivered, suddenly cold.

"Right," Merlin muttered. "Time for a bit of hunting, I think."

The merlin flew up towards the roof and freedom. But as he went, she heard the druid call, "Don't let them leave you behind, Rhianna Pendragon. The message on the back of the collar says you're to carry Excalibur to the North Wall in person. Seems young Mordred's rather more stupid than I thought."

◀◎ 3 ◎▶

Left Behind

Ten days the knights did ride full sore
To the wall across the northern moor
Where pale ghosts in the shadows fight
And a legion vanished overnight.

The meeting broke up soon after that. The knights rushed off to prepare for their journey to the North Wall, leaving Rhianna sitting alone and forgotten in the Great Hall. She touched the carved arms of her chair where her mother's ghostly hands had rested. She even imagined she could smell a flowery scent, though that must be impossible. Queen Guinevere had been a spirit image, summoned by the Sword of Light to Camelot's enchanted table. Her body was still in Mordred's prison.

Tears sprang to Rhianna's eyes when she thought of the chain around her mother's wrist. She felt tempted to use the sword to call Guinevere again, but that would be stupid without anyone there who could deal with her cousin's dark magic. At least they knew the queen was still alive. The knights were right. They must rescue her mother as soon as possible, and maybe she could look for the Lance of Truth at the same time.

Don't let them leave you behind, Rhianna Pendragon.

Well, she wouldn't. But she'd need help.

She found Elphin grooming Evenstar. Her friend's dark curls flopped into his eyes as he brushed his mist horse's shimmering tail. The silver spiral she'd given him for Christ's mass – the pathfinder from the end of Merlin's staff that she'd got back from the shadrake during the battle – dangled from his neck, glinting in the dusty sunshine that came through the high window. Evenstar was enjoying the attention, his head bent round to watch his rider. Rhianna wondered if the mist horse was talking to him.

Of course he is, Alba whinnied, nudging Rhianna with her nose over the top of her stall. *Where have you been? I need grooming, too!*

Elphin looked up. "Rhia," he said quietly, his violet eyes searching hers. "Are you all right?"

Rhianna nodded. "I'm fine. But you've got to help me, Elphin! That message was from Mordred. He's kidnapped the queen, and the knights won't let me ride with them—"

Elphin held up a hand, his six fingers spread. He slipped out of Evenstar's stall to join her. "I know. Hush. Cai's somewhere about, and he's really excited about going with the knights when they ride north."

"Cai's going?" Rhianna was a bit upset that the gossip had got around already. If Cai knew, then by now no doubt half of Camelot also knew that she was meant to stay behind, protected in her tower like a helpless princess.

"Yes." Elphin fiddled with the spiral around his neck. "They want him to carry Excalibur. It's supposed to be a big secret, but Merlin flew in here and told me everything… he's still loose,

I'm afraid. I offered to take him back to his perch, but he said he was hungry after all that magic and was off to hunt in the woods."

In spite of her annoyance with the druid for abandoning them at a time like this, Rhianna laughed.

"He spoke to the knights as well. You should have seen Sir Bedivere's face!" She told him about the merlin flying in to read the message on the collar, and Sir Agravaine being worried that he would foul the Round Table. "Sir Bors still wants to leave me behind, though," she added, sobering again.

Elphin smiled. "Don't worry. Cai's on our side. Just give him Excalibur when the knights tell you to, and I'll take care of the rest."

Rhianna scowled at him. "I'm not giving Excalibur to anyone, and certainly not to Cai!

He'll probably drop it in the first muddy puddle he sees."

"I seem to remember you dropping Excalibur in the mud last year, Damsel Rhianna," a voice said, making them both jump. "Didn't hurt it any."

The human boy has been listening, Alba informed her, flattening her ears as the squire peered over the stall at them.

Rhianna frowned. She had only dropped Excalibur once, when Gareth had knocked it out of her hand after she'd splintered his wooden sword during training – a stupid day she'd rather forget. She had been showing off. She'd grown up a bit since then.

"You'd better do what Elphin says," Cai went on. "'Cause we're riding out first thing, and Sir Bors isn't going to let you come. Him and Sir

Bedivere just had a fight in the courtyard. Sir Bedivere said the merlin had spoken to him in the meeting, but Sir Bors said it was his imagination, and the stupid bird had just got loose. I thought they were goin' to kill each other! They actually drew their swords."

Rhianna's stomach fluttered. "They didn't…?"

"No, of course not. But Sir Bors ain't in a good mood, I'm warning you now. He's talking about making sure you stay behind, putting you under guard in your room so you don't try to follow us."

"If he does that, I'll climb out of the window!"

Her voice, not soft at the best of times, had risen. Some of the other squires, grooming the knights' horses, looked round.

"Hush, Rhia," Elphin said. "It's all fixed.

Just give Excalibur to Cai, and trust me."

Rhianna gave her friend a suspicious look. "Like I trusted you at midwinter?"

Elphin's eyes whirled purple. "I only did that to protect you, you know that."

"Sir Bors is trying to protect me, too. By taking Excalibur from me, the only person who can work its magic, and giving it to Cai here, who doesn't even know how to use a wooden sword. Great plan!"

Cai flushed and mumbled something about it not being his idea.

"Rhia..."

"Just get out," she said. "I need to groom Alba, and I can hardly think with you two idiots breathing down my neck!"

Cai and Elphin looked at each other. But they went.

Alba snorted in relief. *I am glad you made them go. My stall was getting very crowded.*

Rhianna pressed her face into her mare's sweetly scented mane and closed her eyes. Could she trust Elphin? She knew he would never hurt her. They'd grown up together in Avalon, where he'd been like a brother to her. But that meant he might want her to stay behind in Camelot where she'd be safe, just like the knights did.

She clutched her mist horse's mane in frustration. "Oh, Alba, what shall I do?" she whispered.

Just groom me, the mare answered, nudging her. *That joust made me sweat. I have an itch behind my ear.*

Rhianna smiled. Still trying to think of a way to persuade the knights to let her go with them, she obliged the little mist horse by brushing energetically behind her ears.

❀

By the time she had finished grooming the mare, she had a plan. She'd work on Sir Bedivere, who had heard Merlin at the meeting and stuck up for her in the courtyard. She would remind him that only a Pendragon could work Excalibur's magic, and between them they would talk the other knights into letting her ride with them.

Since they were unlikely to listen to a scruffy girl, she climbed the winding stair to the Damsel Tower and let Arianrhod help her bathe and wash her hair. When, after supper, Sir Bors called for her to bring them Excalibur, she felt strong enough to go down and face the knights again.

But to her disappointment, Sir Bedivere was

not there. Instead, Sir Bors had brought two men she didn't recognise, armed with lances. They gave her awkward looks.

"Ah, there you are, Damsel Rhianna!" he said, running an approving eye over her green dress – which was actually getting too warm for the weather but was still her favourite. "Have you brought Excalibur?"

"Yes, Sir Bors," she said, swinging aside her skirt to show him the sword in its red scabbard.

He eyed the sword warily. "Right. You'd better wrap it in my cloak so Cai can carry it safely. Wouldn't want it burning the poor boy, would we?"

Rhianna ignored the cloak he held out to her and rested her hand on Excalibur's hilt. "Since I'll be riding with you tomorrow, I won't need to wrap it."

Sir Bors sighed. "No, Rhianna, I'm sorry but this time you're not getting your way. It's much too dangerous to take you that far north. I know you made a treaty with the Saxon chief Cynric, but there are other barbarians raiding the northern coasts... Jutes and Scots, and God knows what other riff-raff. To say nothin' of your cousin Mordred and his bloodbeards up there in the wilds. No, you stay here with your fairy friend and Arianrhod, where you'll be safe."

Rhianna set her jaw. "The message says I have to carry the sword to the North Wall myself. If I don't go, Mordred won't give up my mother. I know he won't."

The big knight frowned at her. "How do you know the message says you're to carry it?"

"Merlin told me, so there's no use lying

to me. He spoke to you, too, didn't he? I know you heard him! Sir Bedivere heard him as well. He thinks I should go, doesn't he? Cai told us you had a fight in the courtyard, earlier."

"That boy's tongue is going to get him into a lot of trouble one day." Lips pressed tight, Sir Bors tugged the blood-soaked slave collar from his belt. "Did Merlin tell you what else the message said? That we're to hand you over to Prince Mordred with this thing fastened round your neck… I'm not the only one who thinks there's dark magic on this collar. We're goin' to burn it before we leave, so nobody's going to be wearin' it, least of all the Pendragon's daughter!"

Rhianna swallowed. She felt a bit sick. "I'm not afraid," she said. "I'll be all right with Excalibur."

Sir Bors eyed her determined chin and her hand gripping the white jewel. He glanced at the two sentries. "Sorry, Damsel Rhianna, but we really haven't time for this. We can do this easy or hard, it's up to you. But one way or another, you're giving me that sword tonight." His hand rested on the hilt of his own sword.

Her heart thumped. She didn't want to fight the big knight, but she couldn't let him take Excalibur.

Sir Bors was watching her closely. "We're not plannin' on giving Mordred Excalibur, if that's what you're worried about," he said more gently. "We just need it to get close to him and find out where he's keeping Guinevere. Do you want us to be so worried about you we daren't lift a finger to rescue your mother? I know you don't frighten easy, but in this case it's not a question of bravery. It's the queen's life we're talking about."

He laid the cloak on the floor between them and pointed. The sentries watched her sword hand warily.

Rhianna remembered what Cai had said about Sir Bors putting her under guard in the Damsel Tower, and sighed. She had to avoid that, whatever happened. She'd give him Excalibur now and get it back later. Dropping her gaze, she unbuckled her sword belt and wrapped both sword and scabbard in the scarlet cloth.

He picked up the bundle and grunted. "Good girl. Now then, we ride at first light, as you no doubt know, since young Cai seems unable to guard that tongue of his. It's a fair way up to the Wall. Even on good horses without any bother from the Saxons, it's goin' to take us the best part of a month to do the round trip. Sir Bedivere's in charge here at Camelot till we get back. Anything you need, you go to him, understand? But don't pester him. His job is to look after you till we're back here with Lancelot and the queen, or—" He broke off, then added, "We'll rescue her, don't you worry. Mordred's not gettin' away with this."

"Yes, Sir Bors," she said, still meekly.

He gave her a suspicious look. "Right then, off to bed with you. And I want you to stay up in your room in the morning. There'll be a lot of excitement in the stables, horses tramping everywhere. No place for a damsel."

"But I—" Rhianna said, tensing.

The knight motioned to the sentries. "These men will stay outside your door the whole time we're away so you can feel safe."

Rhianna eyed the men, thinking of what Cai had said. Her spine stiffened. "If you think I'm going to stay in my room for a *month*..."

Sir Bors frowned. "Now, now, Damsel Rhianna. Nobody said anything about staying in your room that long. Just till we're out of the way, that's all. A few days, maybe."

"A few *days*? But who'll exercise Alba? She has to go out, and nobody but me can ride her."

"The Avalonian boy will take her out with his horse." Sir Bors frowned at her. "Now be sensible, huh? I'm sure you don't want everybody gossiping about how Rhianna Pendragon had to be locked in the dungeon like a naughty squire to keep her out of mischief."

Rhianna stared at the big knight in disbelief.

"I'll order it, Rhianna," he warned. "Unless

you give me your promise now, on your father's sword, that you'll not ride north after us. Well…? I'm waiting."

She glared at him, too furious at how he'd tricked her to remain meek. "I'm the Pendragon! You should do what *I* say."

"No, Rhianna, you know that's not how it works here. Your father, King Arthur, was one voice among many. He made the Round Table so he'd never misuse his power, and we've voted on this. You and that fool Bedivere are the only ones who seem to think it a good idea that we take you into Mordred's bloodthirsty hills and hand you over to him to do with as he likes. He's already killed your father and got our queen in chains. Even the Romans couldn't handle those wild northern tribes. They built that Wall for a good reason, and you're goin' nowhere near it, even if I have to lock you in the dungeon for the entire summer for your own safety. So do you promise, or do I ask these men to escort you down there now?"

Rhianna felt dizzy at the very thought. She glared at the sentries. One of them gave an embarrassed cough. But they stepped forward, ready to take hold of her arms if need be. Sir Bors held out the bundled Excalibur, its jewel poking out of the end.

She closed her eyes. It wasn't too late. She could snatch Excalibur back, call on the other ninety-nine knights to help her... but this was clearly a test, and she had more chance of getting out of her room than getting out of a locked dungeon.

She took a deep breath, placed her hand on the jewel and looked Sir Bors in the eye.

"I promise not to *ride* north after you," she said through gritted teeth.

She'd walk the whole way, if she had to.

Sir Bors' eyes narrowed. "A Pendragon never breaks a promise. You know that, don't you?"

"And I won't break mine!" Rhianna said, thinking of her cousin breaking his knightly oath to kill her father. "But if Mordred hurts my mother…"

"Good girl." Sir Bors gave her one of his unexpected, gruff hugs. "That little traitor Mordred won't harm a hair of the queen's head while I still live and breathe, I promise you that."

This did not make Rhianna feel much better. She hated to think of the big knight lying dead in the wild northlands, because of her.

❧❦❧

When the knights rode out the next morning, pennants flying from their lances, Rhianna could only watch in frustration from her tower window. Cai trotted proudly in the middle of the troop on his pony, carrying the cloak-wrapped sword strapped to his saddle. The sun had not yet risen, and they soon disappeared over the bridge and into the mist.

She glared at the door. The two sentries still stood outside. She had heard them all night, shifting their feet. One of them had an annoying cough. She wondered when they would sleep. Not soon enough.

She was leaning out of the window to see if Elphin was taking the mist horses out yet, when Arianrhod came in with her breakfast.

"My lady!" Arianrhod dropped the tray on

the bed and hurried across the room to grab her sleeve.

"Oh, stop it," Rhianna said. "I wasn't going to jump, silly. They've gone now, anyway. I just hope they don't get any blood on Excalibur so I can't take it back to Avalon for my father." A lump came to her throat.

The other girl hugged her. "Oh, Rhia… I know you wanted to go as well, but the knights are right. It would have been too dangerous. And it's lovely here in spring. Sir Bedivere's told me to pack a picnic for when you're allowed out, the first sunny day we get. At least if Prince Mordred and his bloodbeards are meeting the knights up at the North Wall, we know they're not terrorising people around these parts."

"I haven't time to go on silly picnics!"

Rhianna frowned at her friend. Then she had a horrible thought. "What if Mordred's planning to attack Camelot while the knights are away in the north with Excalibur? He's sneaky like that, isn't he? If I haven't got my sword, I can't protect you! We've got to go after them, quick."

Arianrhod's lips twitched.

She glared at the girl. "It's not *funny*, Arianrhod!"

"I know, I'm sorry." The dark-haired girl glanced at the door and closed it. She whispered, "But you see, the picnic's just an excuse to get you out of here. We're going to the North Wall as well. Elphin says he can get us there before the knights. I can't tell you any more now. Just don't do anything stupid before then."

Rhianna gripped the girl's wrist in hope. "We're going after them? But Sir Bors made me promise... never mind. Are you sure we'll be there before them? What's the plan?"

"Shh, the sentries will hear you." Arianrhod glanced nervously at the door again. "I don't know what your Avalonian friend is up to, except that it'll involve some magic. We're going to the spiral stones. They've got strange powers." She touched the scar on her cheek and shivered. "Merlin used to take your father there... Lady Rhia, you're hurting me."

Rhianna relaxed her grip, ashamed to see her fingers had left red marks on her friend's arm. "Sorry... it's all the sword training. I forget my own strength sometimes." She took a deep breath and thought of the stones Arianrhod had mentioned. "Do you mean where we camped on our way from Avalon? I had a dream of Merlin there."

She looked at the window. It would be a lot easier to escape her guards on a picnic than stuck inside Camelot. If they were lucky, Merlin might even be there, waiting for them. She smiled. "Oh, all right," she said loudly enough for the sentries to hear. "I'd better go on this picnic, I suppose. At least it'll get me out of this stupid tower! I suppose my faithful guards are coming, too?"

Arianrhod smiled back. "I expect so, and Sir Bedivere's men of course, and probably some of the squires. But it'll be fun, you'll see, even if the magic doesn't work."

When her friend had gone, Rhianna ate her breakfast thoughtfully. She wondered what Elphin had in mind. She needed to talk to him. But when she quietly opened the door that afternoon, hoping the sentries might have fallen asleep at last, they crossed their spears and grinned at her.

"Not yet, Princess Rhianna," they said. "Sorry. More than our lives are worth."

"But I want a bath."

"Your maid will bring you hot water. You've got everything you need up here. It's only for day or two. And Sir Bors said if you try anything stupid like climbing out of the window, we're to take you down to the dungeons for your own safety. So best not try, huh? You'd probably break your neck, any rate."

Rhianna retreated back inside. She checked the drop into the courtyard. An Avalonian could have done it, maybe. But she was human with no magic, and now she didn't even have Excalibur so she couldn't talk to Merlin if he did come back.

✼

The following days were the hardest of Rhianna's life. More frustrating even than her childhood in Avalon, when Lord Avallach wouldn't allow her through the enchanted mists to look for her parents. There, the magic had stopped her from leaving. Here she had two human guards instead, who escorted her about Camelot like a prisoner.

When they let her out of her room on the second day, she almost gave them the slip and galloped after the knights on her mist horse. But she knew Sir Bors would only send her back again, and then Sir Bedivere wouldn't let her go on the picnic, which seemed her only chance now of getting to the North Wall before Mordred got his hands on Excalibur.

To make things worse, she guessed her

friends were not telling her everything. Elphin said they had to wait for Merlin to return, because he needed his help with the magic. Arianrhod kept avoiding her eyes and dropping things, until – infuriated – Rhianna told the girl to get out of her room.

With nothing better to do, she stared out of her window imagining all the terrible things Mordred might be doing to her mother. Day after day passed, with no sign of the merlin. She wondered if the druid knew she was still stuck in Camelot, and tried to persuade her guards to take her out into the woods to look for her missing hawk. But they just laughed and shook their heads. "Nice try, Princess," they said. "Wait for the picnic, then we'll all ride out together."

Rhianna sighed. A fine mess she was

making of her quest! She'd hoped to have two of the Lights by now. Instead, Sir Lancelot had gone missing with the Lance of Truth, and with every day that passed the knights were closer to their meeting with Mordred. She took comfort from Sir Bors' promise that they wouldn't let her cousin near Excalibur until the queen was safe, and prayed Cai wouldn't do anything stupid with the sword until she got there.

DARK AMBUSH

Mordred sat on his horse in the dusk, watching the road below. The animal would not stand still. Every time it moved his bad leg hit the rocks, making him curse under his breath. The knee would no longer bend properly, and his foot stuck out like a broken lance. But soon he'd have two of the Lights in his grasp. Then he'd be on his way to commanding the Grail that could end his suffering.

His heart quickened as he heard the sound of hooves echoing in the pass. His fist clenched on the reins and the horse danced sideways, bruising his leg again. He barely felt the pain. Would Arthur's knights have obeyed his instructions to the letter?

His men came instantly alert and flitted from rock to rock. Mordred had to admire their skill. "At last," he growled. "If they'd taken another route—"

"They had to come this way, Master." His bloodbeard captain, the same one who had let Arthur's daughter slip through his fingers last winter, scrambled down from the lookout. "They were a bit slower than we expected, that's all. Got a pony with them."

"Ah yes, for my cousin to ride – don't suppose she can manage a full-grown horse," Mordred said, satisfied. "Make sure you snatch her when you snatch the sword. And don't let her escape this time."

"Yes, my prince." The bloodbeard's cheek

twitched, showing a new scar, a souvenir from the shadrake that had almost killed him during the battle for Camelot last year. He had as much reason to hate the girl as Mordred did.

"I want her alive," he added, a bit worried that the man might get carried away. "And undamaged."

The bloodbeard's face fell. "What if she puts up a fight? I know she's only a damsel, but she does have your uncle's magic sword…"

"And you have fifty trained fighters!" Mordred snapped. "Plus the advantage of surprise. Do I have to climb down there and snatch her myself? Because if I can do that, I won't need you any more, will I?"

The bloodbeard stiffened. "N-no, Master. We'll get her for you. Alive and undamaged, as you say."

They'd chosen their ambush well, where the old Roman road entered a narrow valley with cliffs on both sides. It was already dark in the shadows below, but enough light remained to show a large party of knights riding up from the south. They looked tired and dusty. Their horses' heads hung low.

Mordred's eye fixed on the dun-coloured pony in the centre carrying a small figure in a hooded cloak. He smiled. Last time they'd met, he had been wounded and helpless while his cousin held a magic blade to his throat. Today, their positions would be reversed.

She rode astride, not side-saddle like most damsels, but he'd expected that. The cloak would be to hide her from curious eyes. He was sure his bloodbeards had reported a white pony… but maybe it was dirty.

Most importantly, he could see a large
sword strapped to the pony's saddle.
The white jewel on its hilt caught the last
of the light. *Excalibur*.

He smiled again. His mother had been
right. Arthur's knights were leaderless and
stupid. They had ridden straight into his trap.
By tonight, they'd all be dead, and he'd have
the Sword of Light and Arthur's daughter.

It was too dark to see which knights had
come. Not all of them, obviously. They would
have left some men to defend Camelot. But
once he had Excalibur, the others would have
to do what he said.

Then his stupid horse flung up its head
and neighed.

The knights, who had been warily eyeing
the cliffs, looked up in alarm and snatched

out their swords. One of them rode out in front with a lance, yelling for the others to retreat.

Mordred cursed as they started to turn their horses. He heard unearthly shrieks and the clash of metal below as his bloodbeards attacked from the rocks. He saw one of his men die on the end of the lance, which luckily jammed in the cliffs before the knight could skewer anyone else with it.

The pony, frightened by the dark figures dropping from above, whipped round. Its rider fell off. He grinned. But it wasn't his cousin. Instead, a plump fair-haired boy scrambled up and ran for the mouth of the pass.

"Tricked! They tricked me... get the sword!" Mordred yelled, seeing his bloodbeards hesitate. "Never mind the boy. I need that sword!"

He dragged out his mother's mirror. Urging the horse up to the lookout rock, he raised the glass to the sky. "Mother, help me!" he called, and flashed the mirror's dark magic at the knights.

Black clouds boiled above him, making his horse rear in fright. Purple lightning crackled down the cliff, dislodging boulders that bounced down into the pass. The knights were forced back.

Mordred laughed. This was more like it.

His captain ran to the terrified pony and grabbed the sword from its pack. The other bloodbeards swarmed back up the cliffs, leaving Arthur's knights turning in confused circles below.

At first he couldn't see what had happened either, and thought his men had made a mess of things. Then the bloodbeard captain appeared with a long bundle strapped across his back, spooking the horse again.

"Bring it here!" Mordred snapped, his eyes on the big white jewel poking out of the end.

The bloodbeard did so, stammering excuses.

"Shut up, will you?" Mordred said, impatient. "So the girl's not with them, so what? We'll deal with her later. The important thing is we have Excalibur! With this, I'll soon get the Lance of Truth off that fool Lancelot, and then we'll teach my cousin and her little friends a lesson they won't forget in a hurry. Hold my horse." He dropped the reins, took a quick breath and drew the sword out of its wrappings with a cry of triumph.

"Careful, my prince…"

"Oh, for Annwn's sake! I'm Arthur's rightful heir, aren't I? It won't harm me."

He felt slightly disappointed that there was no surge of power as he drew the blade. But his cousin had unknighted him, so that would probably come after he got his mother to re-link the sword's magic to his spirit. It felt heavier than he'd expected, too, no doubt because he'd lost his strength over the winter along with his sword hand. But he'd soon get used to fighting left-handed… that would confuse Lancelot.

"*Now* we'll see who's in charge, you fools!" he yelled, pointing the blade after the fleeing knights. "Go on, run back home to Camelot! Did you really think I would just hand over the queen to you? You don't deserve a magic sword. The Pendragon's power is *mine*."

4

Spiral Path

Long ago druids walked this land
Where giant stones in circles stand
And ancient powers there await
Merlin's ghost to open the gate.

Nine days after the knights had ridden north with her sword, Rhianna sat astride Alba in the courtyard impatiently waiting for the guards to open the gates.

Merlin perched on her wrist, wearing

a hood like the other hawks and gripping tightly with his claws. He'd flown back into her room yesterday as if nothing had happened. She couldn't talk to him without Excalibur's magic. But it was obvious the silly bird had been roaming free in the woods, while she'd been escorted about Camelot like a prisoner, having nightmares about what her cousin Mordred might be doing to her mother.

"Ow," she muttered. "Don't hold on so tight. I won't drop you."

To her frustration, their 'picnic' had turned into a major outing. When they'd heard about it, all the squires and damsels wanted to come, and Sir Bedivere had to find extra men to escort them. With so many hungry mouths to feed, the cooks had to pack extra food and drink, and that meant they needed ponies to carry it all.

And then Sir Bedivere insisted they should take King Arthur's pavilion, too, in case it rained. The poles and folded canvas travelled in a wagon drawn by two oxen, which was sure to slow them down still further.

"I don't mind getting wet," Rhianna said, scowling at the cart. "We got wet enough on our way here from Avalon. Anyway, it's not going to rain."

For once, the sky looked cloudless and the sun felt warm on her arms, making her even more impatient to get out of this courtyard. If she had to spend one more day trapped behind walls, she would scream.

"I wouldn't be so sure about that, Rhia," Elphin said. He sat calmly beside her on Evenstar, his harp in its bag slung across his back. "Weather in the world of men seems very unpredictable. Let them bring the tent. We might need it."

"Why?" Rhianna said. "We haven't time to camp, or we'll never catch up with the knights."

"Shh." Elphin glanced at Arianrhod, who rode in the wagon with the other damsels. "It's all taken care of, I promise. Trust me."

Rhianna scowled again. "You've been saying that for nine days already!" But she held her tongue. The last thing she wanted to do was to make her guards suspicious and have them lock her back in her room.

Without Excalibur, she felt undressed. At least she had been allowed to wear her armour and bring her father's shield. Sir Bedivere had actually told her to, in case of Saxon trouble. But he wouldn't give her a replacement sword as well. She saw Gareth – who did carry a sword – smirking at her, and set her jaw.

At last the gates opened, and Sir Bedivere led them out into the spring sunshine. Alba gave a little buck of excitement, nearly unseating Merlin from her wrist.

Let us gallop on the river and leave the humans behind! the mare said.

Rhianna smiled. It was very tempting. Let Sir Bedivere and her guards and the squires and the stupid cart try to follow them! With their enchanted horseshoes that allowed their mist horses to gallop across the surface of water, she and Elphin could be away into the hills long before the others reached the bridge.

Elphin must have read her thoughts, because his hand closed on her rein. "Not yet, Rhia," he said. "Wait until we get to the stone circle." He fingered the druid spiral as he rode, and again she got the feeling he was hiding something from her.

But with the sun shining and Alba prancing under her, it was difficult to stay angry for long. They crossed the bridge and turned on to the Roman road. The damsels and squires laughed and chattered as they rode through meadows full of wildflowers. They passed a village, where the people paused in their work to stare at her. "Princess Rhianna!" they called. "It's the princess!"

She began to feel hot under her armour and thought about taking it off. But after a glance at Gareth and his friends, she changed her mind. If they were attacked, it wouldn't be much use folded across her saddle.

Soon they reached the stone circle where they'd camped last year. Then it had been winter and dark, and a dragon had been chasing them. Today, with the sun shining, it seemed a different place. The air between the stones sparkled slightly, like the air in Avalon. Rhianna's neck prickled as she thought she saw her father's ghost in the centre, beckoning to them. Alba pricked her white ears with interest.

Sir Bedivere ordered the pavilion to be set up inside the circle. The damsels unloaded the food, while the squires took the bridles off their ponies and turned them loose to graze. Then everyone raced off to fly their hawks. The men took up guard positions around the circle.

Elphin had been studying the stones. He glanced at the merlin on Rhianna's wrist and nodded. "Let's ride that way." He headed Evenstar around the hill.

As they passed the stones, the wind dropped and the laughter of the others faded. Rhianna felt dizzy and shook her head to clear it. "Come on, Elphin," she called. "It's about time you told me what the plan is. I've been going half crazy stuck up in my room!"

"I know, Rhia. I'm really sorry we couldn't get you out before, but things took a bit longer than we thought. Arianrhod should be here soon. Ah, here she is…"

The dark-haired girl stepped out from behind a stone so suddenly that Alba *misted* in surprise. Rhianna found herself sitting in the grass, blinking up at her mare's sparkling tail. Merlin, still leashed to her wrist, beat his wings against the ground and screeched at her.

Alba trotted back and sniffed her anxiously.

I am sorry! I thought you could stay on me now.

"That's only when I'm carrying Excalibur, silly," Rhianna muttered. But she wasn't hurt, just embarrassed.

"Then you'd better carry your sword, my lady." Smiling, Arianrhod held out a long bundle wrapped inside an old sack.

Rhianna saw something glitter in its folds. She stopped brushing grass off her backside and stared at the sack in disbelief. "Is that…?"

Arianrhod took the merlin and passed the bundle to Rhianna, who unwrapped it quickly. She sucked in her breath as Excalibur's white jewel blazed in the sunlight. The hilt warmed her hand, familiar and comforting. Hope filled her, and her dizziness vanished.

"Cai and Elphin swapped it for an ordinary one the night before Sir Bors' party rode out," the girl explained. "Cai'll keep the secret as long as he can. By the time they unwrap the sword to check, it'll be too late."

Rhianna let out her breath. She didn't know whether to be angry with her friends, or hug them. "Why didn't you tell me before?"

"We couldn't tell you, Rhia," Elphin said. "You'd have given us away, and then Sir Bedivere would have sent someone after Sir Bors with the real Excalibur. You had to be convincing."

"Oh, I was convincing all right. My guards nearly locked me in the dungeons!"

"I know. They said you were the most stubborn damsel they'd ever had to guard." Arianrhod giggled. "But we'd have got you out again."

Rhianna forgave them. She vaulted back into Alba's saddle, thinking fast. "The knights might not notice if Cai keeps it wrapped up, but the wrong sword won't fool Mordred for long... we've got to go after them, quickly! How long will it take to get to the North Wall? Arianrhod, you'd best tell Sir Bedivere we're flying my merlin down in the trees. That'll give us a head start..."

"Wait, Rhia!" Elphin caught her reins to stop her galloping off. "We don't have to gallop all the way to the North Wall, silly! Besides, you made Sir Bors a promise, so we can't ride north."

Rhianna frowned. She rested her hand on Excalibur's hilt. "My mother's more important than a stupid promise. Let go of my reins!"

"We're not going to ride north after the knights," Elphin continued calmly, "we're going to get there ahead of them. Remember how Merlin brought us through the mists from Avalon?"

"A spiral path," she breathed, realising at last what her friend meant. "And you've got Merlin's pathfinder..."

"Exactly." Elphin smiled. "Merlin tells me the druids used these stone circles to travel secretly in the world of men. There's still power in this one – see how Excalibur shines here? We just need to find a way through the mists to another circle near the North Wall, but we don't want everyone following us, and Merlin's not sure he can close the path in the body of a bird. So after we've eaten and everyone's dozing in the sun, I'll play my harp to make sure they doze a bit deeper. Better keep Excalibur hidden until then."

Rhianna re-wrapped the sword and strapped it to Alba's saddle, next to her father's dragon shield. She thought of the knights' faces when they got to the North Wall to find her waiting for them with Excalibur, and grinned.

❧❦❧

The plan went well enough at first. Nobody objected to Elphin's harp, and that afternoon sweet Avalonian music rippled across the hillside. Maybe because of the stones around them, the magic worked more quickly than usual. Soon, the squires and damsels were asleep on cushions and rugs in the shade of the Pendragon's pavilion. The sentries rested their backs against the stones and dozed off as well. Sir Bedivere, who had been talking to one of them, yawned.

As Elphin's magic filled her head, Rhianna's eyelids started to droop, too.

She saw her father sitting in the pavilion among the sleepers, holding something in his strong hands. As she tried to see what it was, a bright white light surrounded him, and it turned into the splintered head of a lance.

He looked straight at her. "*Mend the Lance of Truth and you'll free Guinevere,*" he said.

"Wake up, Rhianna Pendragon!" Merlin's voice snapped. "Do you want to be left behind again? Let me loose, quickly."

She jumped alert as the merlin pecked her wrist. It had grown cooler. Long shadows from the stones fell across the sleeping sentries. Her father's ghost had gone. Alba waited next to Evenstar, pawing the ground. Elphin was already mounted, playing his harp one-handed, the reins lying loose on his mist horse's neck. The spiral around his neck glittered like a star.

Alba whinnied to her in excitement. *Are we going home now?*

"No, we're going to find the Lance of Truth and rescue my mother," Rhianna told the mare, excited now too. She checked that Excalibur was safe and mounted quickly.

Arianrhod came running over, leading the pack pony. Merlin flew ahead around the circle of stones, following the sun. Arianrhod followed him with a determined expression, whispering to the pony. Rhianna pushed Alba into a trot.

They moved slowly to start with, until they'd completed three circles. Then Elphin slipped his harp back into its bag and urged Evenstar into a canter after Merlin, who had sped up. The sentries stirred as they passed. Squire Gareth woke up and blinked after them in confusion.

"Keep up, keep up," Merlin called. Arianrhod was running now, dragging the reluctant pony. The air around them blurred, and the pavilion with its sleeping squires and sentries disappeared into a sparkling mist. Rhianna clung to Alba's mane and eyed the sky warily, remembering the last time they had followed Merlin through the mists, coming over from Avalon when the shadrake had attacked them.

They completed another circle, before a shout came from behind. "Oy! Where do you think you're going with the princess…?"

Rhianna glanced back and saw her guards staggering to their feet. She wasn't going to let them take her back to Camelot now. She struggled to unwrap Excalibur. The blade gleamed brightly as she drew it, burning a hole in the mist.

"Put that sword away, Rhianna Pendragon!" Merlin snapped. "You'll destroy the magic. Elphin's finding this hard enough as it is."

She quickly sheathed Excalibur, and the mist thickened around them again. But she heard hoof beats coming after them and kept her hand on the hilt, looking over her shoulder. They had lost sight of the stones now. Her hair stood out in a crackling copper cloud. Alba's tail floated like foam. She heard Elphin breathing hard, and Arianrhod give a little gasp.

Then there was a flash of light, and they were trotting across springy heather into a blazing red sunset. The air smelled different. Wind tugged at her hair. And it was *cold*.

Rhianna shivered as they drew rein. She gazed around warily. They had emerged from a circle of mossy stones into drifting mist on a deserted moor. Ahead of them, across a wide ditch, a wall of stone snaked along a ridge. Dark towers rose out of the mist along its length in both directions. A startled stag bounded away, scrambled through one of the crumbling gateways, and disappeared down the slope on the other side.

"The magic worked," Arianrhod breathed, staring around wide-eyed. Her teeth were chattering. Remembering her first experience of the spiral path, Rhianna felt a bit sorry for the girl. But she was glad her friends had come with her.

Then a shout came from inside the circle, and Gareth stumbled out of the stones, waving his sword dangerously. Close behind the squire came Sir Bedivere riding his chestnut bareback, followed by Rhianna's two faithful guards clutching their lances.

Merlin, who had been chasing a rabbit, swooped back.

"Well, don't just stand there!" he scolded. "Get out of that circle and let me close the path before half of Camelot follows you up here!"

The little bird dived back into the stones and vanished in a sparkle of stars.

Rhianna watched the circle anxiously, remembering what Elphin had said about the druid not being sure he could close the path in a bird's body, but nobody else appeared. Nor did the merlin. The last of the mist blew away in crimson rags and the magic died, leaving their little group standing alone on the northern moor.

The men looked at the Wall uneasily. Then Sir Bedivere leaned over to take Alba's reins. Before Rhianna could stop him, he'd dragged the little mist horse back into the stone circle after the merlin.

"What am I going to do with you, Rhianna Pendragon?" he said, shaking his head at her. "I knew you and your friends were up to something, but I never thought you'd try anything as stupid as this! If that's the North Wall, as I think it is, we're in a lot of trouble. All right, fairy boy, you got us here, so you can take us straight back again. Quickly, before anyone spots us."

Elphin clutched his spiral and shook his head. "Sorry, sir, but I don't think I can without Merlin's help."

Rhianna bit her lip. Her friend looked exhausted. She wondered how they were going to get back now the path had closed with Merlin on the wrong side.

Sir Bedivere frowned at them. Arianrhod looked at her feet. Gareth folded his arms with a smug expression. "Are you going to whip her for breaking her promise, sir?"

"If I'd been allowed to go with the knights in the first place, we wouldn't have had to use magic to get here," Rhianna said, glaring at Gareth. "And I didn't break my promise because we rode in a spiral, as you very well know since you were following us, you little sneak."

"That's enough, you two!" Sir Bedivere said. He let go of Alba and took a deep breath. "Let me think. If we can't go back the way we came, then we've got to find shelter for the night. It's too exposed up here." He looked at the Wall again.

"Lancelot's place is somewhere near here, isn't it?" one of Rhianna's guards suggested. "Maybe if we follow the Wall, we'll find someone who can give us directions."

"We're more likely to run into Mordred's bloodbeards if we go stumbling about up here in the dark," Sir Bedivere said. "Best thing we can do is wait for Bors and the others. They should be here soon, and hopefully we'll be able to work something out before we meet Mordred." He looked at Rhianna and sighed. "I *thought* I wasn't imagining things at the Round Table meeting... seems Merlin's just as much trouble in the body of a bird as he was in a man's."

The sun slipped down behind the ridge as they tried to decide what to do next, and it quickly grew colder. Sir Bedivere mumbled something about finding a road. But since none of them had actually been this far north before, nobody seemed to know quite where they were. The men even argued about which side of the Wall they were on, Prince Mordred's or King Arthur's.

"Where did Mordred say to meet him with the sword?" Rhianna asked.

Sir Bedivere gave her a distracted look. "Don't even think about it, Damsel Rhianna. We're in enough trouble, as it is."

But Gareth looked at her with more interest. "That's Excalibur, isn't it?"

For the first time, the knight noticed the bundle tied beside the shield on Rhianna's saddle. He went still. "Don't tell me you... oh, this goes from bad to worse! So which sword's Sir Bors got?"

The friends glanced at one another.

"Just an old one nobody wanted," Arianrhod admitted. "I found a white jewel in the queen's treasure chest about the same size as the one on

Excalibur's hilt, and Elphin used his magic to stick it on."

"You stuck it on with fairy magic?" Sir Bedivere obviously wanted to stay angry. But Rhianna saw the knight's lips twitch. "I'd love to see Mordred's face when he realises!"

"Cai's goin' to be in trouble when Sir Bors finds out, that's for sure," Gareth said with a smirk.

Rhianna wanted to kick the boy, but he was right. Her friends had risked a lot to bring her here with Excalibur. She couldn't let them down now.

In the end, Sir Bedivere decided to camp in the nearest guard tower for the night so that they would be close to the stones in case Merlin came back, and not too far from safety if they had ended up on Mordred's side of the Wall.

They gathered heather, and Elphin played a few notes on his harp to light a fire. Gareth gave the Avalonian boy a look that was half contempt, half respect. Arianrhod unloaded food from the pack pony's bags, and they ate in silence, huddled close to the flames. Sir Bedivere ordered a sentry rota with two men to stay awake at all times. Since they had only three fighting men he included Gareth in this, which cheered the sulky squire up a bit.

Rhianna kept Excalibur near at hand and rested her head on the dragon shield, watching the sparks from the fire fly up through the broken roof of the tower. She felt much too excited to sleep. But the journey along the spiral path must have tired her more than she'd thought. She drifted into a strange dream where the splinters stuck in her father's shield glittered like stars in the sky, and the red dragon came alive to fly up through the hole in the roof, shrieking a challenge.

She looked through the dragon's eyes and saw the dark knight crouched in another of the ruined guard towers below. He brandished the fake Excalibur at her and yelled, "You're going to pay for this, cousin!"

As she tossed uneasily in her sleep, the shadrake that had chased them across the Summer Lands last year flew up out of Mordred's tower, and the two dragons – red and black – fought fiercely in the night sky above the North Wall.

◅◐ 5 ◑▻

The Broken Lance

In the northlands a knight did ride
Searching for his dead lord's bride.
Harp and shield and true words spoken
Can heal the lance that once was broken.

She woke to feel something pricking her throat. The fire had died to a few embers, and the ruin was full of shadowy figures. At first she thought she was still dreaming. Then one of the shadowy figures bent down to lift her hair from her face, and her heart pounded in terror as she realised that the prick at her throat was the sharp end of a spear. She saw Arianrhod held captive by the wall. Another man had hold of Elphin. Sir Bedivere and Gareth had also woken to spears at their throats.

"This one's a damsel wearing armour, sir!" the man standing over her said, lowering his guard.

It was all the chance Rhianna needed. She rolled over, snatched Excalibur out of its bundle and sprang to her feet.

The sword's sudden gleam dazzled her. The man who had touched her hair staggered backwards in surprise, shading his eyes. The men holding her friends captive dragged them further away, while the two guarding Gareth and Sir Bedivere stiffened.

"Drop that sword, damsel, or your friends die!" called a commanding voice from the door.

Rhianna's heart sank as she realised the sentries outside must have been overpowered, too. But having only just got Excalibur back, she wasn't about to let anyone take it from her that easily.

She whirled the blade through the air to make her attacker back off so she could pick up her shield, and retreated step by step until her back met the wall. A glitter on her arm caught her eye. The splinters stuck in the shield were glowing, just like they had in her dream... no time to think about that now.

She put her back to the wall and faced the strangers. By Excalibur's light, she warily checked their faces but saw no blue spirals marking them as Mordred's men. They wore armour similar to Arthur's knights, and they didn't seem to have killed anyone – yet. Their leader was a tall, handsome knight with shoulder-length hair almost as silver as her sword. He took a swift stride towards her, and she tensed. But when he saw the Pendragon shield, he froze.

"Arthur's shield!" he breathed, looking round in confusion. "God's breath, is that Soft Hands down there…?"

"Yes, it's me," spluttered Sir Bedivere from the floor. "You are an idiot, Lancelot! What on earth are you doing creeping along the North Wall like thieves in the night?"

Sir Lancelot.

Rhianna's arm trembled with anger. She gripped Excalibur tighter and took advantage of the knight's distraction to put her blade to his throat. "You let Mordred take my mother!" she said. "Tell your men to let my friends go, or *you* die."

Everybody stared in horror at Excalibur, shining at the champion knight's throat. Lancelot's men started towards her, but backed off when the silver-haired knight raised a hand. Now she had a problem because she could not blood the blade if she wanted to keep Excalibur's magic pure. But hopefully Sir Lancelot didn't realise that.

"I'll do it," she said. "I'm not afraid to use this sword."

"I can vouch for that," Sir Bedivere said. "She fought a dragon and Mordred's bloodbeards with it last year."

"And saw off Lord Avallach's Wild Hunt," Elphin added.

Sir Lancelot gave Rhianna a wary look. "Don't do anything you might regret, damsel," he said. "I want to get the queen back just as much as you do. We're on the same side here." He signalled his men to let Sir Bedivere and the others go. "Truce?"

Sir Bedivere pushed his attacker's lance away and dusted himself off. Gareth scowled and did the same. Arianrhod rushed across to hide behind Elphin, whose harp rippled gently into the night, breaking the tension.

Relieved she wouldn't have to carry out her threat, Rhianna sheathed Excalibur.

While Gareth and Elphin coaxed the fire back to life with a mixture of human skill and Avalonian magic, Sir Bedivere and Sir Lancelot warily clasped hands. Then the men sat down around the fire to exchange information.

Rhianna watched the silver-haired knight with mixed feelings. She hated him for taking her mother all the way to this wild place and letting Mordred capture her. But it seemed that Lancelot and his men were busy searching for the queen. They had been riding along the North Wall day and night, checking every tower and fort, looking for her. When they'd seen the sparks from their fire and the horses grazing outside, they'd thought Sir Bedivere's party were Mordred's men.

"You're lucky we needed information, or we might have killed you first and asked questions later." Sir Lancelot glanced at Rhianna, amused. "The last thing I expected to find was a damsel carrying Arthur's sword! The girl's quick on her feet, I'll give her that. Is she really Guinevere's daughter? You must be crazy bringing her up here so close to Mordred's territory, if she is."

"I didn't have a lot of choice," Sir Bedivere said, giving Rhianna a frustrated look. "I'm afraid Damsel Rhianna was raised in Avalon and has never learned the meaning of fear." He explained about the stone circles and the spiral path.

Lancelot eyed Elphin, who was still softly strumming his harp. "A fairy prince helping men? That's a first. I know Mordred killed Arthur in the battle, but I'm a bit out of touch. Where's Merlin and the other knights of the Round Table?"

"More to the point, where's my mother?" Rhianna interrupted. "Mordred sent us a message saying he'll exchange her for Excalibur, and Sir Bors planned to take him the sword to find out where he was keeping the queen so they could rescue her. But we swapped it, because I need Excalibur for when my father gets reborn."

Lancelot raised an eyebrow. So Sir Bedivere had to explain about that, as well as losing Merlin in the mists between worlds and the druid's spirit ending up in the body of a bird. Meanwhile, the men swapped their own stories, while Arianrhod nervously heated soup for everyone.

More talk. Rhianna wanted to slap the two knights into action, but she supposed there wasn't very much they could do in the middle of the night. Besides, Sir Lancelot and his men claimed they had already checked all the towers between here and the west coast and not found her mother.

Lancelot told them how Guinevere had

been captured on midwinter night and smuggled out of his castle by magic. There had been an eerie sea mist that night, and nobody even realised the queen had gone until the trail was cold. The snow up in these parts had lain deeper than at Camelot, so they had been unable to ride out to look for her. Everyone had been worried about her, though most people thought Arthur's knights had come north and taken her back to Camelot.

Then, when the passes opened again, Sir Lancelot had got a message from Mordred, too – a challenge to joust against the dark knight for the queen's life.

"So it seems Prince Mordred's lying to at least one of us," Sir Lancelot finished, glancing at Rhianna again. "Because he's obviously no intention of letting Guinevere go until he's killed both me and the damsel, and probably not even then, if I know him. Wouldn't surprise me if he's thinking of marrying his aunt to secure his claim to the throne, once we're both out of the way."

Everyone went quiet. The men gave Rhianna sympathetic looks.

She frowned at the silver-haired knight. "But I thought you're supposed to be my father's champion?" she said, her voice loud in the shadows. "You'll beat Mordred easily in a joust! He's only got one hand now. I've seen him…" She thought uncomfortably of the grisly fist the shadrake had stolen away, but surely even the dark magic of Annwn couldn't stick her cousin's severed hand back on again?

"So I heard," Lancelot said. "But not even the Pendragon's champion can fight magic, as you demonstrated so well earlier." He rubbed his throat and smiled ruefully at Sir Bedivere.

"But I'm not going to give Excalibur to Mordred," Rhianna said, still frowning. "So you needn't worry about that. If you're too afraid to ride against my cousin, then I'll joust against him myself!"

Lancelot's men glanced at their leader. Some of them grinned at Rhianna.

"I'm not joking," she said. "*I'm* not afraid."

Lancelot sighed. "I don't blame you for thinking I'm a coward, Princess. Believe me, I'd gladly die a hundred deaths and let the Wild Hunt take my soul, if it would save your mother's life. But you being here changes things. I can't risk duelling against Mordred with a broken lance, and once he finds out you've got Excalibur you'll be in rather more danger than her. So I've got to stay alive for the time being, because you're not going to get very far in these parts with only Soft Hands, a squire and two unmounted guards to look after you."

"Don't forget me and Arianrhod," Elphin said.

Rhianna gave her friends a grateful look. "Have you brought the Lance of Truth with you?" she said, getting impatient.

"I kept it, of course. It's outside on my horse's saddle. But it's not a lot of use now, I'm afraid, not since… it splintered." He seemed about to say something else, but frowned at the fire instead.

Sir Bedivere sighed. "It was your own fault, Lancelot! And now we're all paying for it. The king's sleeping in Avalon awaiting rebirth, while barbarians rampage unchecked up and down the coasts, and the Saxons are more or less in residence in the south. Meanwhile, as if we haven't got enough problems, Mordred's got Guinevere and his greedy eyes are on Camelot. You're going to have to do some fast talking when Bors and Agravaine get up here, I'm warning you now."

"You wouldn't understand," Lancelot said tightly. "You've never loved a woman, have you, Soft Hands?"

Sir Bedivere flushed.

The two knights glared at each other. Rhianna hoped it wouldn't come to a fight. Sir Bedivere would probably come off worse, and she felt a bit sorry for him, having made him come after her through the stones.

Then Elphin's harp rippled out of the shadows, making the fire flame brighter. "I think

I can help," he said.

Everyone looked at the Avalonian boy.

"As I see it, the problem is with the Lance of Truth being broken," he said. "If Sir Lancelot carries the working lance, then no man can best him – true?"

"No man except King Arthur," Sir Bedivere muttered.

Lancelot ignored this. He gripped Elphin's slender wrist. "Can you mend it?"

"Maybe. If I have all the pieces – and if my wrist isn't broken so I can still play my harp."

Sir Bedivere's lips twitched as Lancelot quickly let Elphin go. "It needs a new shaft," the champion knight admitted. "And there's a bit missing off the head. I'm not sure how much. It splintered – I kept all the pieces I could find."

"It's certainly worth a try," Sir Bedivere said. "Gareth, go and fetch Lancelot's bag." Gareth cast a hostile glance at Elphin and ducked out into the night, muttering under his breath about being too old for squire's duties.

Rhianna eyed her friend. "Can you really mend the Lance of Truth?" she whispered. "And if you do, will it help Sir Lancelot kill Mordred?"

Elphin's eyes whirled violet. "I don't know about killing Prince Mordred. But it's one of the Lights you need to bring your father back, isn't it? It won't be as simple as sticking a jewel to a sword's hilt, but I'll do my best." He readied his harp for the second time that day.

The men who had ridden with Sir Lancelot grumbled about needing sleep, not entertainment, and those who had followed

Rhianna through the stones sighed at the mention of more magic. But Gareth emptied the pieces from the bag into Elphin's lap and stared a challenge at the Avalonian boy.

They all looked tired, Rhianna thought. Surely it couldn't be that easy to mend one of the four Lights? They should take it back to Camelot and find Merlin, maybe wait until midwinter again, when magic was at its most powerful in the land of men. Except they didn't have time.

Elphin nodded to Lancelot, who held out his broken lance at arm's length. Rhianna wanted to laugh. The champion knight looked more wary of her friend's harp than he had of her sword.

She sat quietly against the wall with the dragon shield across her lap and picked at the splinters. They glimmered faintly in the firelight, reminding her of her dream when they had formed into a red dragon and flown up through the roof.

As the Avalonian music filled the ruin, the shadows drew back a bit and the men smiled in wonder. The pieces in Elphin's lap began to glow. So did the broken lance. She caught her breath as the light brightened and her friend's fingers moved faster over the strings.

Some of the splinters rose into the air, and Lancelot stiffened. "Keep going," he grunted. "I think it's working…" But even as he spoke the glow faded, and the pieces fell back into Elphin's lap.

He silenced the strings, breathing hard. Sir Lancelot examined the point and shook his head. Rhianna looked at the lance in disappointment. It seemed just as broken as before.

"I'm sorry," Elphin said. "I think some of the pieces might be missing. I can try again later."

"Not here," Lancelot said, gathering the splinters back into his bag and signalling to his men. "If Mordred's bloodbeards heard that, they'll be sniffing around this place come morning. The magic failed last time I used the lance, anyway. I'm not sure I'd trust it against the dark knight. You'd best ride with us until Bors and Agravaine get here. Then perhaps we can make a proper plan to deal with Mordred, as I said we should have done long ago." He gave Elphin a stern look. "And no more fairy music for the time being, or I'll confiscate that harp of yours."

Seeing her friend's eyes darken, Rhianna put her hand on Excalibur's hilt.

But Sir Bedivere covered her hand with his.

"It makes sense, Damsel Rhianna," he said. "We want to get the queen back safely, don't we? And it's a good idea to make sure Mordred doesn't get his hands on any of the Lights, however broken. I never much liked Bors' idea to take him Excalibur. Everything else can wait until after we know Queen Guinevere is safe." He looked meaningfully at Sir Lancelot.

Rhianna wondered what 'everything else' meant exactly. But she relaxed her grip on Excalibur. Sir Bedivere was right. They'd gain nothing by killing each other.

"Sir Lancelot must have trusted magic once," she whispered to Elphin, as they mounted their mist horses. "Or he couldn't have used the Lance of Truth as my father's champion, could he? Something must have happened to make him so suspicious of it.

I wish Cai was here… he'd soon tell us."

Her friend smiled. "Cai'll have quite enough to tell us once he's ridden all the way up here with the knights, as it is. We probably won't be able to shut him up all summer."

Rhianna thought of the lookalike sword strapped across Cai's saddle and felt a bit guilty. She hoped the squire was safe.

><8<

They breakfasted on the last of the supplies. Then they rode east, keeping to the ditch for cover, following the Wall. Lancelot led the way on his big white stallion with Sir Bedivere on his chestnut beside him. Gareth and Arianrhod rode the pack pony, the girl awkwardly clasping Gareth's waist. The squire didn't look very happy about this, but since the alternative was walking he did not complain. Rhianna and Elphin rode their little mist horses in the middle, flanked by her two Camelot guards, while Lancelot's men brought up the rear.

The Wall seemed to go on for ever, winding up and down the ridge. Every mile they came to another crumbling tower like the one where they'd spent the night, and Lancelot sent his men to check it out. All turned out to be deserted, making Rhianna despair that they would ever find the queen. Whenever she thought of that chain on her mother's wrist, her hand tightened on Excalibur's hilt.

Gareth kept looking at her, as if he wanted to tell her something. Finally, when Lancelot and his men galloped off to check yet another tower, the boy held the pony back and said in a sly tone, "If you want to know how Sir Lancelot broke the Lance of Truth and why he's scared to mend it, I saw it happen."

Rhianna stiffened. "How did it break?"

"He was trying to kill your father, of course."

"That's not true!" She halted Alba so suddenly that the little mare threw up her head in protest.

That hurt my mouth, the mare complained. *I will mist if you do it again.*

Gareth smiled. "How else do you think those splinters ended up stuck in the Pendragon's shield?"

Rhianna stared at him, remembering how the splinters had glimmered when the Lance of Truth was near. A shiver of excitement went through her. "Are you saying Sir Lancelot jousted against the king?"

"Ha!" Gareth said. "They jousted all right.

At dawn up by that lake where you found your father's sword. It was misty that morning, so they never knew I followed them. King Arthur rode his golden mare and carried Excalibur. Sir Lancelot rode his big white horse and carried the magic lance. When they met, you could hear the crash back at Camelot."

"How do you know, if you were watching them at the lake?" Elphin said.

Gareth scowled at him. "I know, all right? The other squires told me. Anyway, there was this big flash, like lightning, and the lake went all sparkly. When I could see again, the king lay on the ground and Sir Lancelot was standing over him. But the lance was broken, its head splintered. King Arthur drew Excalibur, and I thought he was going to kill Sir Lancelot. He wounded him, I think. I saw blood on his arm.

But then this woman with long green hair came up out of the lake – stark naked! She must have been swimming in there. While King Arthur was staring at her, Sir Lancelot grabbed the broken pieces of the magic lance, jumped on his horse and got away. Ran back to Camelot to hide behind the queen, like the coward he is."

Gareth smirked at them. "So now you know. I reckon that woman in the lake was your father's secret love, and that's why he never really bothered too much about Sir Lancelot loving the queen."

"Don't listen to him, Rhia!" Arianrhod said, shaking her head. "It's all lies. Your mother and the king loved each other very, very much. Anyway, have you ever seen a woman with green hair? He's just a stupid squire. He doesn't know anything."

But Rhianna knew differently. "It was Lady Nimue in the lake," she whispered, thinking of the fish-lady who had given her Excalibur last year.

Gareth's eyes lit up. "See? What did I tell you? The Lady Nimue… King Arthur's secret love!" Turning, he pushed Arianrhod so that she fell off the pony. The girl rolled down the bank into the ditch with a little scream, while Gareth laughed at her. "Stupid squire am I, witch's maid?" he called. "I can ride better than you, anyway!"

Sir Bedivere, who had been watching Lancelot's men return empty-handed from the tower, approached with a frown. "A knight would not let a lady take a tumble like that, Gareth," he said. "I thought I told you to look after her?"

"She slipped, sir, and she's not a lady anyway. Nobody'll ever marry her with a scar like that."

Arianrhod said nothing. She fingered the pentacle on her cheek and avoided looking at Gareth.

"You can ride with me, Arianrhod," Elphin offered.

The girl gave him a grateful smile, and one of the guards legged her up on Evenstar's hindquarters behind the Avalonian boy.

Alba snorted. *I have told Evenstar not to mist, or the human girl will fall off again.*

Rhianna barely heard. She was still trying to make sense of what Gareth had just told them. Her father and Sir Lancelot had fought over her mother, setting two of the Lights against each other? No wonder the lance had broken! But one thing made sense in her confusion.

"We can mend the Lance of Truth now," she told the knights, "The missing pieces have been stuck in my father's shield all the time."

◄◙ 6 ◙►

Reunion

Oaken grove did shine that night
A beacon calling men to fight.
Old quarrels must be laid to rest
So Lancelot can take the test.

Rhianna tried to persuade Sir Lancelot to try the magic again straight away. But he just galloped off on his white stallion to check another tower whenever she mentioned it, ordering her to stay out of sight. He seemed too embarrassed to talk about it. Sir Bedivere gave her a hug and said he'd never realised the lance had actually broken on her father's shield, and she was clever to work it out.

"Don't worry, he'll do it," Elphin said, staring after the pale-haired knight. "He just needs to get his courage back. I think he's afraid the magic will turn on him again."

Rhianna frowned. She wondered if the champion knight intended to visit every crumbling ruin the entire length of the North Wall, but towards evening he led them off the moor into a wooded valley. They rode in single file along twisty paths and emerged in a small clearing. A single mossy stone stood in the centre. Nearby was a cave, its entrance almost hidden by ivy.

"Oaks," Lancelot said, waving a hand at the trees. "This is an old druid grove Merlin showed us last time he was up here. We've camped here before, and we can risk a fire in the cave. We can at least cut a new shaft for the lance, and it's as good a place as any to try your friend's magic again."

He posted sentries, and they tethered their horses outside. Rhianna's neck prickled as Excalibur's jewel began to glow and the pieces of the lance stuck in her shield sparkled like tiny stars. Light shone from the Lance of Truth, too, haloing Sir Lancelot's hair in silver. "Hasn't done that since Arthur was alive," he muttered.

Elphin smiled and opened his harp bag to show them the strings, which also glimmered faintly. "There's power here," he said. "I think it's going to work this time."

Sir Lancelot nodded. "Let's go inside."

He cleared away some dead leaves that had blown into the cave and carefully laid out all the pieces of the lance.

Elphin told Rhianna to bring her shield. "As I play this time, try using Excalibur to loosen the splinters," he whispered. "I think that'll help." He sat cross-legged and rested his harp in his lap. A gentle chord echoed around the rocks, making her neck prickle again.

The others crowded round the entrance, eager to see the magic working. Rhianna scowled at them. "Careful," she said. "Give us some room."

"You be careful," Gareth said. "We don't want to break Excalibur, too. The fairy boy doesn't really know what he's doing, does he? I bet Merlin wouldn't do it like this."

"Quiet!" Elphin hissed.

Rhianna settled for glaring at Gareth. She felt tempted to give him a tiny cut, just to wipe the smirk off his face – but almost cut Arianrhod instead when her blade slipped on the shield. Sir Bedivere hauled the maid back with one hand and Gareth with the other. He motioned the men to stand back, too.

"Watch your fingers, Damsel Rhianna," he said, sounding worried.

Sweat broke out on Elphin's brow as he played. The pieces of the lance brightened so much that they could no longer look at them, and one of the splinters left the shield and darted into the light. Rhianna felt a surge of energy flow along her arm into the sword. *Mend*, she willed. *Please mend.*

Two more splinters shot from the shield into the light, making Arianrhod give a little scream.

Rhianna smiled. It was working! Elphin's harp sang louder, echoes rippling around the cave.

Then suddenly the air was filled with flying silver darts, which pinged off the rock, making everyone duck. There was a blinding flash and Sir Lancelot yelled in pain. The horses tugged at their tethers in terror, and the men drew their swords and looked round for an enemy.

The music had stopped. Elphin slumped over his harp, panting, his dark curls hanging across his face. Rhianna felt almost as tired as she had done after the battle with the shadrake. She looked eagerly at the Lance of Truth. It lay glimmering faintly in the gloom, whole... no, not quite. Cracks showed in the head where the pieces had fitted themselves together. Even to Rhianna's eyes, it didn't look very strong.

Lancelot frowned at it, hugging his hand,

which had blistered as if he had put it into a fire. "Are you sure you mended it right?" he said. "It doesn't look like it would survive a tilt against the damsel here."

Rhianna clenched her fists.

But before she could challenge the champion knight to test this, a furious voice bellowed from outside.

"It's your own stupid fault Lancelot, you fool! You shouldn't have broken the thing in the first place. We have you surrounded. Get out here at once and hand over that lance, before I skewer you like you deserve."

Sir Lancelot wrapped his cloak around his blistered fingers and grabbed the lance, frowning as the head wobbled. His men, still sleepy from Elphin's music, drew their swords and stumbled towards the cave mouth.

Rhianna dragged out Excalibur, desperately trying to shake off the effects of the magic. If Mordred had found them…

Then a fair-haired squire, not quite as plump as before, ducked under the waving blades and rushed to her side.

"I thought I saw your mist horses!" he puffed. "I guess the spiral path magic must've worked, then? We saw the light shining through the trees, and Sir Bors recognised Sir Lancelot's horse… but I'm warning you now, he's in a foul mood. We're lucky to be alive! Mordred's bloodbeards ambushed us on the road. They took the sword, the sneaks… seems they never meant to exchange the queen for it in the first place… good thing we swapped them, only Sir Bors don't know that yet, of course! You're going to have to tell him,

Damsel Rhianna. Rather you than me... Hey, are you all right?" The boy frowned at her as she swayed in relief. "Sir Lancelot didn't hurt you, did he? Why are Elphin's fingers bleeding?"

Rhianna relaxed. "Cai," she said with a laugh. "Don't you ever stop talking?"

Elphin smiled, too. "Told you we'd never shut him up, didn't I?" he said, setting down his harp. "Rhia, I'm afraid you'll have to handle this. The magic was difficult this time. It felt like something was working against me. I don't think my fingers are up to making peace between Sir Lancelot and the other knights just now."

Rhianna gave her friend's bleeding hands a concerned look. But she'd seen them like that before, after he'd played the Saxon camp to sleep, and they had healed fine.

She turned her attention to the knights.

Things looked tense at the cave mouth. Sir Bedivere stood between Sir Lancelot's men and those who had ridden up from Camelot with Sir Agravaine and Sir Bors. He had his arms spread to keep the two groups apart, and was trying to explain. Meanwhile, Sir Lancelot and Sir Bors glared at each other over Soft Hands' shoulder. They looked ready to kill anybody who got in their way.

She elbowed her way through the men to reach Sir Bedivere's side, raised Excalibur and shouted, "STOP FIGHTING!"

Since they still stood in the mouth of the cave, her voice echoed powerfully around the rocks as Elphin's music had done earlier. Excalibur gleamed brightly in the shadows, and the Lance of Truth glimmered in response.

Sir Bors stared open-mouthed at the sword

shining in her hand. "Damsel Rhianna! What are *you* doing here? And you've got Excalibur! But Mordred took it from us in the ambush... So how...?"

Sir Agravaine pushed forward and scowled at Sir Lancelot. "I don't know what tricks you're playing, or how you got the girl up here when we left her safe in Camelot," he growled. "But you're not going to hand her over to Mordred like you gave him Guinevere! I'll throttle you with my bare hands if I have to."

"He didn't *give* my mother to Mordred," Rhianna said. "Can't you see? He's trying to get her back! And it's a good thing we didn't let you take Excalibur, or Mordred would have it by now and we'd all be in trouble. Lancelot, sir, please put that lance down. Sir Bors, tell your men to put away their swords. Why don't you all sit down around that stone out there and talk about this, like you do at my father's Round Table. Everyone has a voice, right? You told me that's how it works. So Sir Lancelot should have a voice, too."

Her arm trembled from using Excalibur's magic to control the knights, but it did the trick. Sir Bedivere's lips twitched. "Well done, Damsel Rhianna," he whispered. "They wouldn't listen to me."

Sir Bors and Sir Agravaine eyed each other, but stepped aside. Sir Lancelot gave Rhianna a grateful look. He pushed between the two knights, glaring at the Camelot men until they stepped out of his way, too. He propped the Lance of Truth carefully against the druid stone, sat on a nearby stump and folded his arms. His gaze darted warily about the grove as he waited for the others to join him.

Sir Bors sighed and sheathed his blade. "Damsel Rhianna's right. Let's put our differences aside until the queen's safe, huh?" He held out his hand.

Lancelot nodded, and they clasped hands.

Sir Bedivere spread his cloak for Rhianna, and she sat beside him with some relief, while Cai and Gareth went off to settle the horses. Alba misted back through the trees, where she and Evenstar had fled from the flash caused by Elphin's magic when he'd mended the lance.

Is it safe now? asked the mare, laying her soft nose on Rhianna's shoulder and breathing into her ear.

"I think so, beautiful one," Rhianna whispered, sheathing Excalibur at last so she could soothe her little mist horse. "At least they're going to talk instead of killing each other."

>⚜

The men talked long into the night. There was quite a lot of arguing, mainly about tactics for defeating Mordred if he brought an army along with him to the duel. Apparently, this would take place inside an old Roman fortress, where the road passed under the Wall and there was space for mounted knights to tilt on neutral ground.

Rhianna remembered the squires tilting at Camelot, and shuddered at the thought of two grown men carrying full-length lances. Nobody seemed very pleased with Sir Lancelot's explanations of why he had ridden off with Queen Guinevere. But they all seemed to agree that he was the best knight among them, and so should be the one to answer Mordred's challenge.

"If Mordred hasn't got Excalibur, then it won't matter if the lance's magic works or not, will it?" Sir Agravaine said. "If Lancelot can disable the traitor for us, then that'll leave the way open for us to rescue the queen, even if his bloodbeards don't honour the bargain."

"And if Mordred kills Lancelot?" Sir Bors said.

An uneasy silence fell. The knights all looked at the king's champion, his pale hair shining in the moonlight as brightly as the mist horses' coats.

"Then it'll save us the bother, won't it?" Agravaine growled.

Lancelot met their stares defiantly. "If he does, I'll take the witch spawn with me," he said.

"Just promise me you'll look after the queen and get her safely back to Camelot. None of this is her fault."

Sir Bors grunted. "We're not goin' to hurt Guinevere, you fool. She's the girl's mother, ain't she?" He glanced at Rhianna.

The talk turned to the Lance of Truth and whether it would work properly now it had been pieced together. Lancelot got up to examine it again, and muttered something about an oak shaft maybe making it stronger. He sent a couple of men off to cut one.

Rhianna heard wing beats in the night above the trees. She peered nervously up through the branches, remembering the shadrake that had attacked them last year. But it was too dark to see very much, and whatever it was flapped away.

Sir Lancelot frowned at the sky, then knelt by the lance to help his men attach the new shaft. This proved a slow process, with much cursing and arguing. They didn't have the right tools, but were making do with a battleaxe and their daggers. Sir Bedivere had nodded off, his head against the stone. Sir Bors and Sir Agravaine muttered together in the shadows, casting the occasional glance at Rhianna.

Something pecked her hand, and she looked down with a scowl to see a small hawk. It fixed a bright eye upon her and cocked its head. She couldn't see the colour of its feathers in the dark, but her heart gave an extra beat as she recognised the shape of its wings.

"Merlin?" she whispered in relief. "Is that you?"

He had lost one of his jesses, but otherwise

looked unharmed. She quietly put her hand on Excalibur's jewel so she could talk to him.

"Of course it's me, silly child. Why didn't you wait for me?"

"We did wait! But Sir Bedivere wanted to find Sir Bors and the others, and then Sir Lancelot came..."

"Fools, the lot of 'em," grumbled the bird, hopping on to her wrist. "Young Elphin's magic was bright enough to light up two worlds! If Mordred's not seen it, goodness knows what else has. What do you think you're up to, Rhianna Pendragon? I agreed to help your friends bring you here so you could use Excalibur to rescue your mother. I didn't say anything about trying to mend the Lance of Truth! Carry me over to the horses. We can talk there."

"But that's why we had to mend it." Rhianna explained about the duel as she carried the merlin over to the trees, where her friends were rolled in their cloaks, fast asleep. "Did you know about Mordred's message to Sir Lancelot?"

"Can't be in two places at once, can I?" Merlin fluffed his feathers.

Alba sniffed at the bird. *He says his wings are very tired. He has been flying around the spiral path for a long time.*

Seeing the sentries coming her way, Rhianna patted her mare.

They smiled at her. "Bored with all the talk, Princess?" one said. "They'll be up all night arguing, I'll bet. Your father was the only one who ever got anything done around here."

"*I* got things done, you mean," Merlin said,

giving the man's wrist a peck. "Arthur wouldn't have known where to start without me."

The sentry sucked his hand. "I'm glad to see you've got your falcon back, Princess, but you've got to learn to control the bird. Where's its hood?"

"I left it in the stone circle at Camelot," Rhianna admitted. "I didn't think I'd be needing it again."

She hid a smile as Merlin glided from her wrist to perch on the withers of Lancelot's white stallion. The big horse fidgeted and laid back its ears, but didn't throw him off.

"Hmm, so this is what it feels like to sit on a champion's horse," the druid said. "Very tall."

Rhianna squeezed through the other horses and frowned at the bird. "If you just came here to peck people, I'm going back to sleep," she hissed. "I had to use Excalibur to help Elphin mend the Lance of Truth, and then to stop the knights killing Sir Lancelot, and you know how the sword feeds on the Pendragon's energy. I'm tired."

"No doubt that's why you're so grumpy tonight," Merlin said. "I only peck people if they don't listen, so pay attention! If Lancelot wants the lance's magic to work for him when he meets Mordred, then he's got to carry it with the right reason in his heart. You'll have to tell him, since he can't seem to hear me in this bird's body."

"He wants to rescue the queen... isn't that the right reason?"

"Yes and no," said Merlin in his cryptic way. "*Why* does he want to rescue her? That's the question."

Rhianna sighed. She felt too weary to think about it. "To save her from Mordred, of course. The same reason I do, so she'll be at Camelot for my father when he returns."

"Really? I can't see into Lancelot's heart, child, and nor can you. Just make sure you tell him what I said before the duel. Only he can know what's in his heart when he rides against Mordred... though we'll find out soon enough, and if the lance doesn't work for him then I expect I'll have to sort everything out, as usual." He sighed. "As if things weren't difficult enough when I had my druid's staff to help people out of sticky corners like this one. We'll just have to hope your Avalonian friend made a good enough job of mending the thing."

Rhianna frowned at the druid. "Can't you help Elphin mend it properly?"

"You think I'd dare meddle with one of the four Lights, do you, Rhianna Pendragon? Even if I still had my druid's staff and my old body, I wouldn't have that kind of power." Merlin shook his head impatiently. "No, no, if Avalonian magic can't mend the Lance of Truth, nothing can, and we haven't time to try again now anyway. The duel's set for tomorrow, and it'll take you that long to ride up to the fort and secure your position. Young Elphin did well. The lance looks whole enough for the purpose. Its magic should work, provided whoever carries it has a true heart! Talk to that fool Lancelot. He doesn't listen to many people, but you're Guinevere's daughter so maybe he'll listen to you."

"Maybe not," Rhianna muttered, thinking of how the she'd put Excalibur to the champion knight's throat earlier. She opened her mouth to ask what reason Sir Lancelot *should* have in his heart when he jousted against Mordred. But just then the white stallion put down his head and gave a huge buck, sending the startled bird flying through the trees, flapping his wings for control.

Rhianna couldn't help a laugh.

"I hope you're not laughing at me, Rhianna Pendragon!" Merlin called as he righted himself in midair and flew off into the night. "Got things to do. I'll meet you back at the stone circle."

"Which one?" she called. "When? Where are you going *now*?"

But the merlin had already vanished into the dark.

Probably off after another mouse, Rhianna

thought with a sigh as she quietly rejoined her friends. Without waking them, she lay with her back against Elphin's, for warmth, and her head resting on her father's shield. She tucked Excalibur inside her cloak in case of trouble. But with so many knights around them, she felt safer than she had since leaving Camelot.

Although tired, she couldn't sleep for thinking of meeting her cousin Mordred again. She wondered if he'd be as handsome as the shadowy versions of himself he'd sent using dark enchantments to scare her last year. Or would he be the crippled one-armed boy she'd met at midwinter when she'd taken the spiral path to his lair – if she'd actually *gone* there in the flesh, and it hadn't just been a dream brought on by Merlin's magic... Well, tomorrow she'd find out.

She tried to pick up the knights' discussion again, though the men's voices had quietened so she couldn't hear all the words. She heard her name mentioned a few times. But eventually, the knights stopped talking and settled down to sleep. She thought about creeping across to tell Sir Lancelot what Merlin had said. But before she could bring herself to leave the warmth of her cloak, she dozed off into a muddled dream of her cousin Mordred galloping towards her in his glittering black armour with the Lance of Truth aimed at her heart.

❦

She woke with a start, her back cold, to find the sun slanting through the trees. Half the men were already on horseback. Elphin was saddling the mist horses.

She sprang to her feet and looked anxiously for Sir Lancelot, but there was no sign of the champion knight or his white stallion.

"Where's Sir Lancelot?" she said. "I've got to talk to him…"

"Don't worry, Damsel Rhianna," Sir Bedivere said, catching her arm as she hurried towards Alba. "Lancelot and Bors have gone on ahead to spy out the fort. Agravaine's still here with half the men. We're to ride after them, and then if Mordred's up to any tricks, at least he won't get hold of you or Excalibur."

"But I've got to see Sir Lancelot before the duel!" Rhianna said, thinking of what Merlin had told her. "It's very important. Has he taken the Lance of Truth with him? We don't even know if the magic will work yet…"

Sir Bedivere smiled and tweaked her messy

braid. "Trust me, Rhianna, we know what we're doing. Arthur himself taught us the arts of war. Yes, of course Lancelot's taken his magic lance with him. But we've got Excalibur, and your friends are all here – look, here's Arianrhod now. She'll sort you out with some breakfast."

"I haven't time for breakfast!" Rhianna said. "You don't understand."

The knight gave her a sympathetic look. "I know you're worried about your mother," he said quietly. "But things are going to work out just fine now we've got Lancelot back on our side, you'll see. Prince Mordred'll soon have second thoughts, once he realises we've joined forces against him – and we have you to thank for that. I think old Bors is glad you're up here with Excalibur, even if he acts like he's not. But you've got to be sensible and let us deal with Mordred now. This joust isn't going to be a little tumble for fun, like the squires' tilt. It's a duel to the death."

Dark Tricks

Mordred halted his horse and frowned around the old fort he'd chosen for the duel against Lancelot. It had started to rain, turning the grass to sticky mud. His bloodbeards crawled over the walls, making things ready for tomorrow. They kept looking nervously to the south, where last night the sky had lit up like a beacon. Some mischief caused by Arthur's knights, no doubt. But they couldn't do much without Excalibur.

"No, no!" he shouted, as his men began to stack arrows above the archway that led south to his Uncle Arthur's lands. "Not there, you fools – Lancelot will see them, and then he won't come inside alone."

"But Master!" said his bloodbeard captain. "That's the most vulnerable spot. What if he brings an army with him?"

"That's why you're here, isn't it?" Mordred trotted his horse into the shadowy archway under the Wall and aimed a kick at the bloodbeards. They scattered, wary of his temper since he'd realised the trick with the boy in the cloak.

He wasn't surprised his cousin hadn't brought the sword north herself. No doubt she was too scared. But he couldn't understand why its jewel remained so dull and cold. It had always blazed brightly whenever King Arthur drew Excalibur. Had she got her fairy friend to put a spell on it?

He checked no one was watching, and

pulled out his mother's mirror. As he peered into the dark glass, the temperature dropped and the rain turned to sleet. His horse fidgeted uneasily.

"Mother?" he whispered. "Are you there? You'd better link my spirit to Excalibur now, in case Lancelot comes early."

Her image swirled to life, its beauty spoiled by a frown as she examined the sword hanging at his hip. "That's not Excalibur, you fool of a boy! Why didn't you contact me before? I think we have a problem."

Mordred turned cold. "What do you mean, it's not…?" He stared at the white jewel that looked so much like the one on his Uncle Arthur's magic sword, and felt faint. He clenched his good fist on the reins, imagining they were around his cousin's neck.

"The sly little vixen! That's why I can't feel its power, isn't it? She's sent me the *wrong sword*!"

Did she think he wouldn't notice? Of course, if he hadn't needed to rely on his men to snatch it in the ambush, he might have noticed the swap sooner. He almost wished he had let the knights bring the sword all the way to him now. Then he'd have had an excuse to kill the lot of them.

"Mordred!" snapped his mother. "Are you listening to me? I said we have a problem."

"Yes, it's called my cousin," Mordred agreed. "She's still got Excalibur, so what? At least she's not here. When I've killed Lancelot and the Lance of Truth is mine, I'll ride to Camelot and make the stupid knights surrender. Then I'll deal with her and get the sword as well. She's only a damsel, after all."

"You'll do no such thing!" the witch hissed. "Are you a complete fool?"

Mordred stiffened. "At least I'm still *alive*."

"And don't forget you wouldn't be, if not for my magic!" she snapped. "So you'd better not disappoint me, my boy."

She no longer looked so beautiful. Shadows writhed in her hair, and her eyes flashed black in the glass. He bit his tongue, afraid of her power.

But she sighed and said, "Listen, and listen well. The knights have mended the lance somehow. I don't think it's as strong as when it was made, and I doubt Lancelot can use its magic unless he's had a change of heart since the last time he tried, but you must be very careful. Strike first and make sure you unhorse him. Once he's on foot, he'll have

to drop the lance and fight you with his
sword. He might be fooled by your lookalike
Excalibur long enough to give you the
element of surprise."

A chill went down Mordred's spine.
"But nobody's ever unhorsed Lancelot in
a tilt, except King Arthur that time when the
lance broke…"

"Pull yourself together, boy," the witch
snapped. "I'll help you, of course. Now show
me that sword they gave you."

Mordred reached automatically for the hilt
with his missing right hand. He scowled as
his empty gauntlet flapped against the fake
jewel. Gripping the mirror against his saddle
with his knee, he drew the blade left-handed
to show her.

She was silent a moment. Then she said,

"I sense Avalonian magic in this, but there's no enchantment on it now. It'll do once you've sharpened it. When I've gone, you'll see a snake. Get your men to milk it, and use its venom to poison the blade. There's more than one way to kill a knight."

Mordred swung the lookalike sword, feeling a bit more confident. It was a good enough weapon, well-balanced even if not magic, and he had to admit that it looked the part. Hopefully Lancelot would not be able to tell the difference, either. He looked forward to seeing the champion knight's face when he thought he was fighting against the Sword of Light.

"Where's the queen?" asked his mother, interrupting his thoughts. "I trust you haven't been stupid enough to bring her down here?"

Mordred smiled. "No, she's still tucked up safe in her tower. I left the spirit channel to your mirror open so she can watch the duel."

"You're a soft-hearted boy," his mother said, more fondly now. "Good. Between us, we ought to be able to deal with Lancelot. His two weaknesses are his knightly code and his love for Guinevere. He won't do anything to endanger the queen's life. Now then, put that mirror where I told you, and leave the rest to me."

Mordred obediently reached up and wedged the glass in a crack above the archway that separated his lands from his Uncle Arthur's. A chill green mist breathed along the Wall, making his bloodbeards shiver. The mist curled around the ruins, and a shimmering green curtain filled the archway behind them. Beyond it, thunder rumbled, and a black snake slithered out of the shadows. The horse leaped forward with a surprised snort.

Despite his injuries, Mordred hardly moved in the saddle. The animal would jump like that at the start of the tilt, and he'd been practising. Admiring the way the green light reflected in the jewel of the Excalibur lookalike, he ordered his men to catch the snake.

So Lancelot had stupidly mended the Lance of Truth to bring to this duel? Mordred laughed. He was ready to take it from him.

7

The Duel

Annwn's shadow guarded the gate
Where a daring knight met with his fate.
Not mirror dark, nor sword, nor spear
Could scare a damsel with no fear.

To the death. A shiver went down Rhianna's spine. She wanted to yell at the knights for being so stupid as to have duels to the death in the first place. She hated to think what might happen to her mother if Sir Lancelot lost.

They rode along the secret road that followed the ditch, keeping out of sight of the Wall. It was badly overgrown, and thorns caught at their hair and clothes. Sir Agravaine grumbled the whole way. He kept giving Rhianna suspicious looks over his shoulder, no doubt to check that she and Elphin hadn't vanished into a magic mist while he wasn't looking.

As the banks rose on each side, Cai scared them with stories of how Mordred's blood-beards had blocked the road with an avalanche, swooped down on them while they'd been busy clearing the rocks, and made off up the cliffs with the sword before the knights could even get their horses out of the pass to follow them. "Sir Bors said they must have really wanted to get hold of the sword, or else they'd have stuck around to kill us all," he told them in excitement. "They used their dark magic to get down the cliffs without being seen, and there was this great hailstorm with stones as big as my fist and purple lightning! We couldn't see nothing! I thought they were going to murder me…"

"Wish they had," Gareth muttered. "Then at least we might get some peace and quiet around here." But the older boy had been listening to Cai's tale as eagerly as the rest of them. He looked a bit jealous that the squire had been part of such an adventure.

"But weren't you carrying the sword, Cai?" Arianrhod asked, her eyes wide. "How did you escape?"

"Yeah, how come you're not even hurt?" Gareth said. "Or did you just hand it over, all nice and innocent like?" He made his voice high and excited like a small boy's. "Here, Prince Mordred, *please* take Excalibur, I've carried it all this way north just for you…"

Cai glowered at him. "Just remember I knocked you off your horse once, Gareth," he said. "I can do it again."

"Oh stop it, you two," Rhianna said impatiently. "That sword they took wasn't Excalibur anyway, so it doesn't matter, does it? My mother's more important." She kept thinking of the queen in chains in Mordred's dark tower. To make things even more miserable, it had started to rain. Elphin rode beside her, huddled under his cloak. He had knotted his reins so he wouldn't have to hold them with his blistered fingers. "Do they hurt very much?" Rhianna whispered to her friend.

"Can you still play your harp?"

He gave her a small smile. "If I need to," he said. "Don't worry, I'll help Sir Lancelot all I can."

Cai admitted he'd left the sword tied to his pony's saddle while he went to help with the rocks. "I thought they were going to take poor Sandy, too," he said, patting the pony's shaggy neck. "Only he stuck in his toes and refused to move, so they just grabbed the sword and left him."

Stubborn Saxon pony, Alba snorted, making Rhianna smile.

"Been cleverer if he'd kicked those blood-beards to death like a proper knight's horse," Gareth muttered, but not very loudly. He still rode the pack pony, although Arianrhod had accepted a lift on the supply wagon the knights had brought north with them so she wouldn't have to ride double with the boy. Rhianna didn't blame her.

While her friends swapped stories, she tried to think how best to get Sir Lancelot to listen to her. But, to her frustration, before they caught up with Lancelot and the others Sir Agravaine led them south off the road to a ruined villa whose gardens stretched down to the river.

"Bors said to stay out of sight," he explained. "If there's trouble, he'll send a messenger."

Rhianna stopped Alba and looked back the way they had come. She could just see an arched gateway, where the Roman road passed under the Wall heading north. A track led across the moor to meet it.

"Don't even think about it, Damsel Rhianna!" Sir Agravaine growled, grabbing

Alba's reins. "Get down off that fairy horse right now, and be sensible for once. We might still have Excalibur. But until we know exactly where the queen is, and how many men Mordred has brought with him to this duel, we can't risk an all-out battle with his forces. If he's made new allies in the north..." He and Sir Bedivere exchanged worried glances. "Our best hope is that Lancelot manages to kill the traitor."

"Can't we watch?" Gareth said, trying to see the fort, his eyes shining. "It should be a good fight."

Rhianna clenched her fists. "Don't any of you care about my mother? You don't understand! If I don't speak to Sir Lancelot before the joust, *he's* the one who's going to get killed, and then Mordred will come after us, anyway."

But it was no good. Short of galloping off to the fort alone – which even she had to admit would be stupid with Mordred's bloodbeards swarming all over it – there wasn't much she could do until Sir Bors and the others came back.

She dismounted with a sigh. She tried to tell herself that she was worrying about nothing, and soon Sir Lancelot would come riding into the villa with the queen sitting behind him on his white stallion and the Lance of Truth shining proudly in his hand. Then the knights would see off Mordred's forces, Merlin would be waiting for them at the stone circle, and they'd all return safely to Camelot with her mother and the two Lights, where she'd find her father's ghost waiting to congratulate her on completing the second stage of her quest…

Horse comes! Alba warned, pricking her silver ears.

Heart racing, Rhianna stared through the broken gates to the north. It had stopped raining, and wisps of mist rose from the river to hide the moor.

"Is it Lancelot's stallion?" she asked the mare.

Not the white, Alba said. *He is trapped in the between place.*

Before she could work out what her mare meant, one of Sir Bors' men came galloping through the gates on a sweaty horse, shouting for Sir Agravaine. "Prince Mordred tricked us!" he said. "He's brought an army with him, and the queen's not with them, as far as we can tell. Lancelot's insisting on jousting with Mordred, anyway. But there's some kind of dark magic at work up there. Bors says to bring Excalibur…"

"Told you, didn't I?" Rhianna shouted. She vaulted back on to Alba, glad she hadn't unsaddled the mare. Calling for Elphin to follow, she drew her sword. "Take me there. Now!"

Sir Bors' man looked startled at her commanding tone. But seeing Excalibur gleam in the mist, he nodded and turned his tired horse.

"Wait, you fool!" Sir Agravaine said. "The damsel's not in charge here."

Rhianna set her jaw. If he tried to stop her this time, she'd fight. But he looked at the blade shining in her hand and sighed. "We're coming, too."

They rode at a gallop across the moor, the knights' horses thundering beside the two mist horses. *This is fun!* Alba said, flattening her ears at the stallions. Cai and Gareth urged their ponies after them, determined not to be left behind. Arianrhod stayed at the villa with the wagon and the two faithful sentries who had followed them from Camelot. Rhianna hoped they'd look after her friend as well as they'd guarded her.

The ruined fort Mordred had picked for the duel perched on the ridge, open to the sky. Its walls framed a rectangular area with two entrances – an archway on their side leading through the Wall, and a gate leading north at the other. Mordred's men had removed stones from the inner divisions and used them to block the other gates, so the only way in or out was through one of those entrances. Beyond the fort, in the valley north of the Wall, they could see smoke rising from many campfires.

More worrying still, above the fort hung a glimmering green mist. Shadows writhed and twisted inside it, reminding Rhianna of the souls the Wild Hunt had taken after the battle for Camelot last year. The green light filled both entrances like ghostly gates.

She shivered, and Alba flared her nostrils. *Smells bad.*

Sir Agravaine swore under his breath. "Looks like a whole tribe of the devils over there! Where's old Bors got to? And what's that green stuff?"

"It's got thicker since I left," said the man who had come to fetch them. "That idiot Lancelot went charging inside without us, and nobody else could get in… Bors was trying to when I came to fetch you."

"Magic from Annwn," Elphin said. His eyes

whirled purple as he looked at the glimmering curtain blocking the gate.

They could hear the clash of swords from the other side of the Wall, interrupted by grunts of effort. Every so often a cheer went up, and the shadows in the green mist cackled and hissed.

Two of Lancelot's men came galloping along the Wall to meet them. "Thank God you're here!" they said to Sir Agravaine. "Lancelot's in trouble in there – but we can't get inside to help him! Bors has taken his men east to look for another way round. He says we're to hold this entrance so Mordred's lot don't come through and jump them from behind, and you're to take your men west till you find another gate and meet him on the other side. There's a whole bunch of them wild bloodbeards in there with their prince, and God only knows what else." He eyed the green mist and crossed himself.

"Nearest gate's at the last fort," Agravaine said, thinking aloud in battle mode. "A mile back, unless we can get over the Wall before then. We could climb it once we get out of sight of Mordred's sentries, but we'd be powerless against that lot on foot... our strength is in our speed and our horses, and we can't leave the youngsters unguarded on this side."

"We could come with you," Rhianna said.

"Absolutely not." He gave her an exasperated look.

"Maybe a few of us could climb over, sneak into their camp, find the queen and bring her out?" one of Lancelot's men suggested.

"If she's even there, which I doubt..."

While the knights argued their next move,

Rhianna gripped Excalibur's hilt firmly, took a deep breath and quietly trotted Alba towards the ghostly entrance. She was about to tell the little horse to mist, when something flashed in the arch overhead, making the mare stop dead.

This is a bad place. Alba flattened her ears and snorted. *I do not want to go in there.*

"Nor do I," Rhianna told her. "But we've got to, or we'll lose the Lance of Truth to Mordred, and he might kill Sir Lancelot, and then he'll hurt my mother." She still blamed the champion knight for letting Mordred kidnap her mother, but they needed him to win this duel.

She peered through the rippling green curtain, trying to see the shadows struggling on the other side. No bloodbeard seemed to be near the gate. She quietly made a hole in the mist with Excalibur and caught her breath.

Inside the fort, under a ghostly green roof, Sir Lancelot duelled fiercely with a knight dressed from head to toe in glittering black armour. She could see at once it wasn't a fair fight. The dark knight was still on horseback, whereas Lancelot fought on foot. His white stallion stood riderless, pressed against the wall, sweating and trembling with fear.

Mordred!

Rhianna stared at her cousin, shivers of hatred going down her spine. He rode a black stallion, with one of his legs sticking out at an awkward angle. He'd tied the reins to the stump of his right arm, which ended in a flapping black gauntlet. His left hand wielded a sword that looked exactly like Excalibur, except that its jewel reflected the green light.

Lancelot was fending off the dark knight's blows with his shield raised over his head. Each time Mordred's sword came down, the champion knight grunted and staggered. Rhianna couldn't see the Lance of Truth and hoped it hadn't broken again.

The bloodbeards inside the fort seemed intent on the duel and hadn't noticed her yet. But she was running out of time. Glancing back, she saw Gareth tug Sir Agravaine's sleeve and point at her. Elphin came cantering after her on Evenstar, dragging his harp out of its bag and shouting something she couldn't hear.

As she looked anxiously for her mother, Mordred kicked Lancelot's shield aside and thrust his sword between a gap in the knight's armour into his shoulder. Sir Lancelot roared in pain and dropped his own sword.

Blood dripped down his arm as he fell to his knees clasping the wound.

"No!" Rhianna shouted, gathering up her reins and giving Alba a hard kick in the ribs.

"Rhia, wait—" Elphin called behind her.

His words cut off as the mare leaped bravely into the green mist. The air around them darkened and cooled, and the sound of the fight faded. Riding underwater must be a bit like this, Rhianna thought. Then a long, thin shadow twisted down out of the arch towards her and formed into a dark-haired woman with eyes black as midnight. "I see you, Pendragon girl," the shadow hissed. "You may not pass."

Rhianna shuddered.

"We'll see about that!" She slashed at the shadow with Excalibur. "Get out of my way!"

The sword passed right through the shadow,

which became long and thin again and fastened itself to Alba's tail. The little mare kicked and squealed in terror, then misted under her. Rhianna felt herself falling and grabbed for the mane.

"I don't know who you are," she said determined to stay on. "But you're not really here, are you? This is just spirit magic."

The shadow-woman laughed. "Just spirit magic? How little you understand, Pendragon girl! I'd have thought a child raised in Avalon would be wiser than that. You've no idea how the world of men works, have you? Coming all the way up here with your young friends and Arthur's has-been knights, thinking to get past my spells and rescue your queen! You won't get her even a day's ride home before my son catches you."

My son. Rhianna froze. But it made sense. Who else would be helping Mordred with dark magic?

"You're Morgan le Fay!" she whispered, chilled. "But you're supposed to be in Annwn now."

"That's right." The witch smiled. "That mirror you see up there is my spirit channel. It's connected to your mother's prison at the moment so she can watch my son kill her foolish lover, Lancelot. Shall I let you see her tears when it happens? Or maybe you'd prefer to visit me? A girl should get to know her aunt."

Rhianna looked up and noticed a black looking-glass wedged into the arch above them. It made her head spin. Now she could no longer see the way into the fort, only those writing shadows all around her. She turned Alba in a circle, confused. The green mist became thicker and colder, until she could barely breathe. Shadowy hands clutched at her from all sides, grabbing her ankles and twisting themselves into Alba's mane – though they stayed well away from Excalibur as she swung the sword around to make them let go, at the same time trying not to cut herself or the mare.

I am frightened, said Alba, trembling. *We are neither here nor there. We might be stuck in this green mist for ever.*

Rhianna shuddered at the thought and felt a sudden hopelessness. Mordred was killing Lancelot in there, protected by dark spells of Annwn. She and her friends were out-numbered. The queen was a prisoner in an enchanted tower. Even if they did manage to rescue her, they still had to get her all the way back to Camelot with Mordred's army on their heels…

She heard the witch laugh. But just as her arm started to tire, Elphin's harp tinkled through the mist. The shadows hissed and whirled upwards, sucking back into the mirror. Now that she could see it properly, her stomach gave a jolt of recognition. It was the same mirror Mordred had used to show her the dragon that was attacking Camelot, when she'd travelled around the spiral path to challenge him last winter.

Alba whinnied in relief as Evenstar misted into view beside them, his silver coat shining with the magic of Avalon. Rhianna had never been so happy to see her friend. If they hadn't been on horseback, she'd have thrown her arms around him and kissed him.

"This way, Rhia," Elphin said, catching her reins and turning his horse.

"No, wait… I think I know what's casting the spell on the fort." She reached up with Excalibur and levered the mirror out of the crack. It fell into her lap, flashing darkly.

As she grabbed it, noise exploded around them. Mordred's men lined the walls of the fort, cheering and making bets on the outcome of the duel, just as the squires had done during the spring joust at Camelot. Lancelot was still fighting on his knees but tiring fast. As Mordred raised his sword over the wounded knight's head to deliver a death blow, the green mist began to drift away. Lancelot's stallion raised its head and whinnied to their horses in relief.

The bloodbeards nearest the entrance whirled round to stare at them in surprise.

"Hey!" one demanded, blinking. "How did you get in here?"

Elphin played his harp faster, making the bloodbeards yawn, while Rhianna thrust the mirror into her belt and urged Alba past them towards the duallists.

"Where's my mother?" she yelled, making Mordred fumble his stroke.

His sword knocked off Lancelot's helm. The champion knight scrambled clear of the black horse's trampling hooves and blinked at Rhianna through the blood running into his eyes.

"Beware... took Lance..." he gasped, before collapsing face down in the mud.

Mordred raised his blade again over the prone knight.

Without thinking of the danger, Rhianna galloped Alba between the duellists and brought Excalibur up in a shining arc. It struck Mordred's sword in a shower of stars, and the Excalibur lookalike snapped off at the hilt and went spinning away into the mud. The magical force knocked Mordred sideways. He should have fallen off, except that his crippled arm was still tied to the reins, which had tangled about his shield. His horse spooked and carried him towards the northern gate, where more bloodbeards had run up from their camp to help their prince.

At the southern gate, Sir Agravaine and Sir Bedivere finally arrived with their men, and galloped their big horses through the arch, yelling war cries.

"Well, don't just stand there!" Mordred roared as his men tried to push him back into the saddle. "Pass me that lance and come with me… That was stupid, cousin!" he called over his shoulder. "Now you'll never find the queen, because only I know where she is."

Realising her mistake, Rhianna dragged Alba's head round, meaning to put Excalibur to her cousin's throat and *make* him tell her where her mother was. But there were too many bloodbeards at the northern gate. They had already given the Lance of Truth to Mordred and were running back down to their camp in the wake of his black stallion.

"Rhia, I think he's in a bad way…" Elphin jumped off Evenstar to help Sir Bedivere with the groaning Lancelot, while Sir Agravaine and his men rounded up the remaining bloodbeards, who had been trapped in the fort when the knights arrived.

She gave the wounded champion a distracted

glance but he didn't look as if he'd die. She stared after the disappearing dark knight, one thought only in her head. She had to get to her mother before Mordred did.

"Come on, Alba," she whispered. "I need you to race for me now."

She sheathed her sword and headed the mare towards the northern gate.

"Damsel Rhianna, wait…!"

Sir Bedivere's plea fell on deaf ears. Thinking of her mother chained in Mordred's dark tower, Rhianna was already galloping through the gate and down the slope into the northlands.

Sir Agravaine clubbed the final bloodbeard on the head. "Well, hurry up, then!" he yelled. "Go after her! I just hope Bors has had time to get into position, because otherwise that crazy girl is going to get us all killed."

◁ 8 ▷

Rescue

In prison high the queen did weep,
Afraid her lord would ever sleep.
Then a damsel drew the Sword of Light
And challenged Mordred's men to fight.

As Alba galloped down from the ridge, Rhianna could think only of finding her mother before Mordred spirited her away again. The way was steep and rocky, and she had to concentrate on her riding. By the time they reached the bottom, her cousin had disappeared on his black stallion, leaving his camp in confusion.

Bloodbeards scattered from her path as she swung Excalibur in a gleaming arc. She heard Elphin and Cai calling behind her, and Sir Agravaine's knights pounding after her on their big horses, but did not slow down. If they caught up, they would only try to stop her.

"Faster!" she called to the mare. "Faster!"

Alba flattened her ears in excitement. *We will win this race.*

Rhianna smiled grimly and risked a look back. Behind her, Sir Agravaine's men were slashing at ropes and felling the standards that stood before the tents. More bloodbeards ran out, armed with axes and bows. Arrows began to hiss around her. She ducked, remembering the arrow that had knocked her off Alba's back when the Saxons had captured them last year. Her Avalonian armour had saved her life back then, but she had fallen off and lost her horse in the mist. That would help no one.

Coming to her senses, she slowed the mare and took shelter behind an outcrop of rock to wait for her friends.

A breathless Elphin caught up first, Evenstar misting to avoid a stray arrow. He gave her a relieved look. Then Cai charged up on Sandy, bringing down another tent as the pony's legs caught in the ropes. "Oops," he said, catching hold of the mane. "He can't do that fairy trick, sorry."

"You carry on," Elphin said, eyeing the struggling lumps under the cover in amusement. "Looks like you and Sandy are doing a fine job of conquering Mordred's army all by yourself."

Cai patted the pony and grinned. "He's nearly as good as your harp."

Rhianna frowned at the boys. "This isn't a game! My mother's still in danger – which way did Mordred go, did you see?"

They shook their heads. Back in the camp, men were fighting for their lives. But here among the rocks it was eerily quiet.

"Then we'll just have to find him another way." Rhianna took a deep breath and pulled out the mirror she'd taken from the arch.

Elphin's eyes whirled violet. "Be careful Rhia," he warned. "That's a thing of Annwn."

"I know what I'm doing. Be quiet a moment." She rested a hand on Excalibur's jewel and warily looked into the mirror. Shadows writhed in the glass, but the witch did not appear.

"I command you in Excalibur's name to

show me where Mordred's keeping my mother!" she said.

The mirror reflected back her freckled cheeks, flushed from the chase, and for a moment she didn't think it was going to work. Then the shadows cleared, showing her the tower room they had seen at the Round Table.

The queen lay on her bed, hugging her chain, her hair in tangles and her eyes red. She was weeping. A bloodbeard poked her with his spear, grinning.

"Prince Mordred has killed Lancelot," he said. "We have the Lance of Truth. Soon we'll have your daughter, too. She's come north with the knights and the Sword, just as our master ordered. Seems she must care about you, after all."

"No…" The queen lifted her chin. "I will not let him use me to get to my Rhianna."

Suddenly, she lurched forwards and made a desperate grab at the bloodbeard's spear.

Rhianna gasped. "No, Mother!" she shouted. "He's lying! Lancelot is still alive."

The queen flinched and stared around, wide-eyed. "Who's there...?"

Rhianna's heart lifted. She could hear her! Then the shadows writhed back across the scene, and the mirror went dark – but not before she'd seen the lonely tower that was her mother's prison.

Fixing the image firmly in her mind, she thrust the mirror back through her belt and took up Alba's reins.

"We've been looking in the wrong place," she told the others. "The tower's that way... it's not part of the Wall at all! Quick, before Mordred moves her."

The boys glanced at each other but did not waste time asking how she knew. When she closed her eyes, the path stretched like a glittering black snake across the moor. They crossed a boggy area, the mist horses keeping their feet dry, though Sandy sank to his knees and splashed Cai with mud. She led the way up a bleak, rocky hillside into the mist – and stopped in confusion.

"It should be here," she said, staring around in despair. Had the mirror tricked them?

Elphin tugged out his harp. As the Avalonian music tinkled across the hillside, the air *shimmered* and they saw the tower, standing up on a rock with green mist curling around it. Rhianna gripped Excalibur tighter and sent Alba cantering up the slope towards it.

She was a bit afraid that they would find Mordred waiting for them inside. But there was no sign of her cousin's black stallion. Two bloodbeards guarded the entrance, stamping their feet and warming their hands over a fire. Elphin led them around the back way, still playing his harp, while Cai untied the guards' horses and shooed them away down the hill.

I have told them the grass is greener in the next valley, Alba snorted. *They believed me.*

As they trotted up to the entrance, the guards whirled in surprise. "Where did you spring from?" one said, blinking at them. "There's an enchantment on this tower. Nobody's supposed to be able to see it."

"*Prince Mordred sent us to keep the queen company*," Elphin sang, magic in his voice.

The bloodbeards exchanged a glance. They shook their heads. "Nobody's allowed in here on pain of death. Prince Mordred's orders!"

"You must be very tired of being stuck up here, guarding her... why not have a rest?" Elphin sang. He carried on playing, until the men yawned and curled up by their fire.

As soon as their eyes closed, Rhianna dismounted. Heart thudding, she pushed open the door and stepped warily into the tower. No torches had been lit inside, but Excalibur blazed brighter than any flame. She raced up the stairs, with Cai and Elphin at her heels.

Another bloodbeard guarded a locked and bolted door at the top. When he saw Rhianna, he grabbed his spear. But Elphin's music enchanted him too, and he slumped against the wall. Cai unhooked the keys from the unconscious guard's belt and opened the door.

Rhianna pushed past him, all caution forgotten.

The queen lay on the bed hugging her chain, exactly as Rhianna had seen her in the mirror, with her dirty hair tangled across her face. She had been dozing. But when they entered the room, her eyes snapped open and she sat up straight. She blinked at the sword in Rhianna's hand.

"Excalibur!" she whispered. Her gaze rose to Rhianna's face, and she blinked again. "I must be dreaming."

"Mother..." Her throat closed. All those years growing up in Avalon she'd looked forward to this moment, and she didn't know what to say.

"*Rhianna*!" The queen went very still, her eyes going wide. "Oh God, I *thought* I saw you at the Round Table, and I heard you speak to me when they told me Lancelot was dead...

but what are you doing here? Did Mordred capture you, too?" She stared fearfully at the door, where Elphin stood with his harp and the echoes of magic on him.

"Lancelot's not dead, Mother," Rhianna said, a choke in her voice. "They lied to you. But he's badly hurt, and Mordred's still around somewhere, so we have to get you out of here right now!"

The queen shook her head in wonder. "My daughter, all grown up and back from Avalon with Excalibur!" She looked at Cai and Elphin. "And accompanied by a squire and a fairy prince. It's like something out of a song." She frowned. "You're not one of Merlin's tricks, are you?"

Rhianna grinned. "No, Mother," she said. "We've come to get you out of here. Hold still, I'll have to cut your chain."

Cai held the chain taut. Praying it wouldn't harm the sword, she raised Excalibur over the horrid thing and brought the blade down with a clang that echoed through the tower. The links parted easily in a shower of sparks. The queen stretched her arm in relief and winced as Rhianna helped her stand.

She braced herself for a hug, hoping her mother wouldn't embarrass her. But Guinevere stumbled to the window and peered out. "Is Lancelot here, too?"

Rhianna fought down a pang of jealousy. "No, I'm afraid he was too badly wounded to come, but we'll take you to him now. I hope you don't mind riding double?"

Her mother drew a deep breath and nodded. She made her way stiffly down the stairs, leaning on Cai's shoulder. When they emerged, she looked in confusion at the snoring bloodbeards and the two mist horses standing with the pony. "But where's your army?"

"They'll be here soon," Rhianna said, hoping it was true.

She helped her mother up on to Sandy, behind Cai, and they made their way back towards the Wall. They went as fast as they could, but her neck prickled and her hands sweated the whole way. She kept expecting Mordred to gallop out of the mist with the Lance of Truth and challenge them. She knew it was only a matter of time before the guards at the tower woke from Elphin's enchantment and raised the alarm, and they still had to get back through the fort.

They were about halfway to the north gate when bloodbeards raced up from their camp to cut them off. Rhianna sliced Excalibur through the air to make a cage of light around them. But more of Mordred's men appeared and drove them back, trapping them against the wall. She cast a desperate look at the stones behind them, but the Wall was high here and the ground rose steeply to meet it. Jumping it would be impossible. Elphin's fingers danced faster and faster over the strings of his harp as he tried to enchant the increasing number of enemies surrounding them.

Their leader pushed his way to the front and bared his teeth at them. With sinking heart, Rhianna recognised the bloodbeard captain who had captured them last year and almost made her blood Excalibur in the battle. She'd thought the shadrake had killed him. She could see the scars made by its talons under his blue warpaint.

"Someone fetch Prince Mordred!" he ordered. "Tell him we've caught his slippery little fish." He turned his attention to Rhianna. "And you be careful waving that sword about, damsel. You might cut yourself."

"I'll cut *you* if you come any closer!" she yelled back.

The queen raised her chin to glare at the men over Cai's shoulder and called in a clear voice, "I order you to let us through! Prince Mordred has no right to keep me here! I am Queen of Britain, so this is treason."

The bloodbeards laughed. "You're queen of nothing now King Arthur's dead."

Rhianna rode Alba forward. "King Arthur's not dead, and I carry the Sword of Light that was forged in Avalon! By Excalibur's name, I command you to let us pass."

The sword blazed. She felt the energy surge along her arm. The bloodbeards eyed it uneasily, but did not stand aside.

"Your magic doesn't work on us, lassie," said the captain. "We'll not obey Excalibur until it is in the hands of our master Prince Mordred, the true King of Britain."

"Rhia," Elphin whispered. "I'm going to try misting through them. The knights can't have gone far. I'll fetch help. Stay here and look after the queen. I'll be back as soon as I can."

The bloodbeards frowned at the Avalonian boy as he trotted Evenstar towards them, calmly playing his harp.

"And your fairy magic don't work on us, either…" the captain began. He covered his head with a shudder as Evenstar misted around him. The little horse misted through the other men as well, neatly avoiding their weapons, and galloped away across the moor.

"Go, Elphin!" Cai yelled, grinning.

But Rhianna shivered. Without her friend at her side, she felt very vulnerable. She moved Alba closer to Sandy and held Excalibur ready for an attack.

I can mist like that too, Alba offered. *You will not fall off me if you carry the shining sword.*

"No," Rhianna told the mare. "Sandy can't mist, and I'm not leaving Cai and my mother here in danger."

The queen frowned at her. "If you can escape like your friend, go!" she hissed. "Otherwise Mordred will just capture us both."

"No," Rhianna said again, setting her jaw. "I came here to rescue you. I'm not going to let anyone take you prisoner again."

The captain, who had been following their conversation, grinned. "Mother and daughter... how sweet! I can see Prince Mordred's going to have a lot of fun with you two later."

Cai scowled at the man. "If that sneak so much as touches a hair of Damsel Rhianna's head, I'll kill him!"

"Oooh!" The bloodbeard captain laughed and raised his hands in mock fright. "So this plump little squire's your new champion, is he? Let's hope he has better luck at it than Sir Lancelot did... is he dead yet? Mordred poisoned his blade before the duel, you know. A small precaution, since you sent him the wrong sword. Once he's killed your fairy friend, he'll be up here to deal with you."

The queen sucked in her breath. Some of the fierceness went out of her eyes.

Poisoned! Rhianna thought of the way the champion knight had sagged under Mordred's final blow. She saw a tear roll down her mother's cheek, and anger filled her. Her fist tightened on Alba's reins. She wouldn't just wait here for her cousin to recapture her mother! If she had to blood Excalibur's blade to help them escape, then so be it.

With a wild cry, she aimed the Sword of Light at the bloodbeard's mocking grin and dug her heels into Alba's sides. "Mist all you like, Alba!" she shouted, as the mare leaped towards their enemy with a fierce squeal.

"Wait, Rhianna!"

Cai's warning came from a long way off. She could barely see through the blurred shadows, and she was concentrating too hard on staying in the saddle to worry about the squire. On all sides, men were scattering and falling to the ground. Her arm ached with swinging Excalibur as she called on the power of the sword to give her strength. Blood sprayed her cheeks. Had she killed anyone? She became aware of ghostly knights on pale horses fighting all around her. From the corner of her eye, she thought she saw her father mounted on a golden mare, bareheaded and wearing silver armour.

"Bravely done, daughter," he said.

Her heart burned with pride, and the sword shone brighter still. Alba's dainty hooves misted through the rest of the bloodbeards without touching them and carried her down the slope into their camp, looking for more of the enemy. She'd kill them all! And then she'd find her cousin Mordred, take back the Lance of Truth and kill him, too...

"Rhia, *enough*!" Elphin appeared at her side on Evenstar. Her friend's six-fingered hand touched her arm, and the ghostly knights disappeared.

She blinked to clear her head, relieved to see him alive. "Those bloodbeards said Mordred's sword was poisoned… I thought he'd kill you!" she gasped.

"You know better than that, Rhia. Avalonians can't die, remember? This way."

They galloped through the wreckage of the camp, half misting, half jumping over fallen tents and the glowing remains of campfires. Horses seemed to be everywhere, some loose, others ridden by knights chasing their quarry. Quite a few of the shelters were on fire, making Rhianna's eyes sting. In the smoke, she recognised Sir Bors' men, who had finally arrived to attack the camp from the other side. Bloodbeards raced in all directions, yelling in alarm as burning brands were thrown into the tents and their belongings trampled.

"My mother!" she said. "Cai! I left them up by the Wall…"

"They're fine," Elphin said, his eyes whirling deep purple. "They're with Sir Lancelot's men."

He led her back to the ruined fort, where to her relief they found Queen Guinevere and Cai with the men who had stayed to look after Lancelot. Her mother gave her a look of equal relief, but quickly turned her attention back to the wounded champion, who lay on a stretcher made from a cloak and two lances. When Rhianna and Elphin joined them, the men picked up the stretcher and hurried through the southern gate to safety, leaving Sir Bors' and

Sir Agravaine's troops to finish off Mordred's bloodbeards.

※

They crossed the ditch, and after a ride that seemed to last for ever reached the old villa where they had left the wagon and Arianrhod. As they pulled up in the overgrown garden, Rhianna flopped over Alba's neck and closed her eyes in relief. She felt a bit sick.

"Did I kill anyone?" she whispered, afraid to look at Excalibur.

She heard the men dismounting. Someone helped the queen down from Sandy's back. Others went to look for firewood to warm the wounded knight. Arianrhod rushed over. "My lady! Rhia! Are you all right? You're not wounded, are you...?"

"She's fine," Elphin said. "She just fought off Mordred's entire army single-handedly, as usual. Let her have a moment to catch her breath."

Rhianna had caught her breath. But she still couldn't make herself look at the sword. "Did I blood Excalibur?" she asked again.

"No, Rhia, the knights did all the killing," Elphin said gently.

"But you were pretty frightening!" Cai said, coming to join them. "You looked exactly like King Arthur used to, when he led the knights against his enemies."

She opened her eyes and turned the sword slowly, examining it for the merest trace of blood. But the blade looked clean. She breathed again, and sheathed it with shaking hands. "I didn't blood it," she said. "I wanted to, but I didn't."

Elphin pressed his lips together. "You have Alba to thank for that," he said. "She misted through those bloodbeards, so your sword must have done as well."

"You should have seen their faces!" Cai said, grinning. "I just turned Sandy round and trotted away with the queen while they were still rubbing their eyes and gaping at you. They never even noticed we'd gone till we were back inside the fort with Sir Lancelot's men."

You felt very secure that time, Alba added.

Rhianna patted the mare and managed a smile for her friends. Then Arianrhod asked, "Did Sir Lancelot kill Prince Mordred, then?" and she remembered her quest.

While the boys told her friend about the duel and the rescue of the queen from the dark tower, she looked back at the Wall in frustration. "We haven't won yet," she reminded them. "Mordred took the Lance of Truth. Did you see where he went, Gareth?"

The older boy shook his head. "Nope, but I hope the knights take him alive. Then we can chain him up in the dungeons and torture him till he tells us where it is."

"Drag Prince Mordred all the way back to Camelot with us?" Arianrhod said with a shudder. "He's bound to work some dark magic on us and escape."

"We won't have to drag him all the way back, stupid. We'll get the fairy boy to take him through the stones, same way we got up here." Gareth smirked at Elphin.

Rhianna eyed her friend. He seemed exhausted, leaning over his mist horse's neck. She wondered if any of them would be able to get back along the spiral path, let alone with an unwilling prisoner.

"They probably won't catch the traitor, anyway," Cai said cheerfully. "And the magic lance must still be broken, or he'd never have got it off Sir Lancelot in the first place. So there's no need to worry, is there, Damsel Rhianna?"

She thought of her cousin galloping off into the mist with the Lance of Truth. *Was* it still broken? They would need to ask Sir Lancelot to be sure, and the champion knight was in no state to talk to anyone. "I hope it's not working," she said. "Because if it is, Mordred's got as many Lights as we have."

◄◙ 9 ◙►

Dark Mirror

The road lay long across the moor
Where Arthur's knights did ride before
Through stone and circle they may fly
But none escape the mirror's eye.

While they waited for the knights to rejoin them, Elphin got out his harp and played a healing tune for Sir Lancelot. Everyone was tense, jumping at shadows. Lancelot's men wanted to take the queen and the wounded champion back to their castle on the west coast. But Sir Bedivere said no, they must get Guinevere to Camelot as soon as possible.

Rhianna watched the Wall anxiously. Would the knights catch Mordred and get the Lance of Truth back? What if the dark knight tried to use the lance's magic against them?

She pulled the dragon shield into her lap and ran her hand over the scars left by the splinters. If she could find just one left behind by Elphin's magic, then at least they'd know the lance wasn't properly mended... but she couldn't concentrate. The effort of rescuing her mother caught up with her, and her eyes closed.

"You've failed," whispered a voice in her ear. "Your champion is dying. My son's got the Lance of Truth."

She tried to sit up, but found she could not move. A shadow bent over her. With a shudder, she recognised the witch from the mirror.

"See how hopeless your quest is?" Morgan Le Fay said with a smile. "Best give up now."

"Not while I've still got *this*…"

With an effort, Rhianna moved her hand to where Excalibur lay at her side. Her fingers touched the white jewel, and warmth flowed up her arm.

The shadow drew back a bit. The witch glanced down and frowned. "Ah, yes, the Sword of Light. It should be in my son's possession by now. But you'll soon give it to him, I think."

"I… will… not," Rhianna said through gritted teeth.

The witch laughed. "So very stubborn! Well, I suppose the Pendragon blood runs in your veins, too. It won't save you, though. You were stupid to come here. You won't get back to Camelot alive…"

Rhianna jerked awake to the sound of men's voices. Someone bent over her. Excalibur was in her hand. Still trapped in her dream, she swung the blade at the shadowy figure.

"Get away from me!" she yelled.

Arianrhod jumped clear in alarm. "Shh, Rhia! It's only me. I came to tell you Sir Bors and Sir Agravaine are back."

Rhianna blinked around warily, looking for the witch. But Mordred's mother had gone. She shivered. It had turned cold, and the light was almost gone. Steaming horses snorted and stamped their feet in the dusk, while the battle-weary knights stood around the unconscious Lancelot and argued.

Something in Arianrhod's hand caught the firelight – the dark mirror she'd taken from the fort. "You dropped this, my lady," she said, holding it out.

She eyed the mirror uneasily. Had it power over her dreams? "Put it in the wagon," she said. "I'll only break it."

Arianrhod slipped the glass obediently into her pack.

Rhianna sheathed Excalibur with a shudder. That had been too close. She had nearly cut her friend! Maybe she should make sure the sword was out of reach next time she slept? Except that might be exactly what Mordred's witch-mother wanted.

"Where's Elphin?" she asked.

"Talking to his horse, I think. The music stopped a while ago. Maybe you should talk to

Alba, too? They seem frightened by something."

"Later. Did the knights get the lance back? I need to talk to them..."

"And I want to talk to *you*, Rhianna Pendragon!" growled Sir Bors, striding across and tugging off his helmet. His hair was stuck to his head with sweat and blood splattered his breastplate, but to her relief he seemed unhurt. "Bedivere's told me all about your little escapade at the tower," he continued. "From the sounds of things, it's a miracle you're still alive. Why can't you just do as you're told for once and stay out of the fighting like a normal damsel?"

"It's not a miracle," Rhianna said. She tilted up her chin and rested her hand on Excalibur's hilt. "Mordred was busy. I had Excalibur, Elphin had his harp, and we were riding mist horses. Besides, I'm not a normal damsel, am I? I'm a Pendragon."

"A dead Pendragon before much longer, if you go on like this." Sir Bors shook his head at her. "Your father had Excalibur and Pendragon blood, too, and look what happened to him!"

Rhianna bit her lip, thinking of her father's body lying in Merlin's boat.

The big knight sighed. "All right, let's see if we can't get that idiot Lancelot and the queen back home to Camelot before Mordred turns up again. We might have a chance of getting through those druid stones of yours, if we travel under cover of darkness. They're a bit close to the Wall for my liking, but if it saves us ten days on the road then it'll be safer in the long run."

"Didn't you catch Prince Mordred then, sir?" Gareth asked, frowning.

"No!" Bors scowled. "He's slipperier than a greasy spear. Vanished once he saw the battle was lost. But he'll not dare attack us again so soon. We've chased his bloodbeards back into their hills. As long as we stick together and stay on this side of the Wall, we should be safe enough. He won't get his hands on your mother again, Damsel Rhianna, don't you worry."

Sir Bors gave her another of his unexpected hugs that squeezed half the breath from her body, then strode off shouting at his men to lift Lancelot's stretcher into the wagon. Rhianna grinned. He stank of smoke and battle. But then so did she.

Sir Agravaine didn't bother telling her what he thought. The tall knight's glower as he went in search of something to eat said it all. It seemed Sir Bedivere was in trouble, too, for letting her come in the first place. This made Rhianna feel bad. Soft Hands could hardly have stopped her, short of locking her in the dungeon at Camelot – although, after being forced to watch her mother fussing over Sir Lancelot, she almost wished he had.

They set out for the stone circle as soon as the knights had snatched a few quick bites and put out their fire. Now Sir Lancelot had been hurt, even Sir Agravaine seemed to have forgiven him for riding off with the queen. "Prince Mordred used dark magic to capture her," the knights muttered to one other. "It wasn't Lancelot's fault. He tried his best to get her back."

Guinevere travelled in the wagon with Lancelot, who still showed no sign of coming out of his fever, while Arianrhod helped her tend the knight's wounds. The other men rode escort along the banks of the secret road, their swords loose in their scabbards and their eyes wary.

Rhianna rode knee-to-knee with Elphin just behind the leading group, worrying about the lance. She kept glancing at her mother, who had Lancelot's head in her lap and was stroking his pale hair. The jealousy came back – she wanted that hand to stroke her hair.

"Give your mother a chance," Elphin said, watching her. "She hasn't seen you since you were a baby. It must be a bit of shock to find her baby daughter all grown up and swinging a magic sword!"

"I know," Rhianna said. "It's just… I thought it would be different, somehow."

"Maybe she'll have more time for you when we get back to Camelot."

"Maybe." She sighed and turned her attention to her other worry. "Can you open the spiral path if Merlin doesn't turn up?"

"I'll try my best. We might still have to ride back the long way, only I'm not sure Sir Lancelot would survive the journey. The knights are talking about leaving him in a monastery until he's stronger."

Rhianna's heart gave a leap of joy at the thought of having her mother all to herself. Then she immediately felt bad. "Can't you heal him with your harp?"

Elphin's eyes darkened. "Mordred's blade was poisoned, Rhia. It's going to take time. It'll be easier if we can get him back to Camelot. Anyway, if Merlin said he'd meet us at the stone circle, he'll come. I expect he's there already, waiting for us, perched on one of the stones eating a mouse and grumbling about us being so slow."

She had to smile. "Will the magic work on so many of us?"

"As long as the path stays open long enough, yes, I think so."

"You *think* so?"

"I've only done it once," Elphin reminded her. "But we'll get the queen and Sir Lancelot through first, don't worry. Then if some of the knights get left behind, they can always ride back the way they came. Best not talk till we get there. Mordred's still out there, remember?"

Rhianna glanced uneasily up at the Wall, which made a black line across the ridge against the stars. Was her cousin up there now, watching them? The thought chilled her, and they rode through the rest of the night in silence.

❧

It was nearly dawn by the time they reached the circle. The ancient stones loomed out of the mist as half-seen silhouettes. The men who had ridden north with Sir Bors and Sir Agravaine blinked uncertainly at them. Rhianna called hopefully for Merlin, but could see no sign of the little falcon. She rested her hand on Excalibur's hilt with a sigh. She just hoped Elphin could remember how to work the magic.

"Right, where do you want us all, lad?" Sir Bedivere said, trying to cheer everyone up. "Be good to get out of this mist! I bet it's a beautiful spring day at Camelot."

Rhianna glanced at Elphin. The circle wasn't going to be big enough for all of them at once. She didn't see how they could repeat the method they'd used to get here, when they'd ridden out in a spiral from the centre.

Her friend thought a moment. Then he rode Evenstar to the nearest stone, spread his six fingers against its mossy surface and reached under his tunic for the druid pathfinder. "We'll need to ride in a spiral *towards* the centre to get back," he said. "That'll reverse the magic. Everyone should follow me as closely as possible... but I'm not going to be able to close the path behind us. That needs magic, and Merlin's not here yet so we'd better hope nobody tries to follow us."

He looked at Rhianna, who drew Excalibur and reined Alba to a halt.

"I'll stay at the back," she said. "I've got one of the Lights, so maybe I'll be able to close it if we need to?"

The knights glanced at each other uneasily. The queen looked up with a frown, but a groan from Lancelot distracted her. Sir Bedivere was trying to explain to the others about the merlin. Sir Bors started to shake his head. But after scanning the deserted moor, Sir Agravaine grunted, "I'll stay with the girl. Let's do this thing as quick as we can, before any of Mordred's bloodbeards turn up."

When everyone was in position, Elphin rode Evenstar slowly around the circle, following the spiral path towards the centre. Behind him went Sir Bedivere with the queen's wagon, flanked by Lancelot's men. Cai and Gareth followed, quiet for once, with Sir Bors' men. Agravaine's men hung back with Rhianna and watched the Avalonian boy in awe.

She smiled as the air around Elphin began to sparkle.

Are we going home now? Alba said, staring after Evenstar with pricked ears.

"Yes, beautiful one." Rhianna patted her mist horse, then realised that the mare probably meant Avalon and said, "We're going back to Camelot, where we'll be safe."

She watched her friends and the men who had ridden north disappear, one by one. It took some time. A wind got up and moaned around the stones, making her shiver. They were going to get wet if they didn't hurry. She was about to tell Sir Agravaine to get going, too, when Excalibur's blade gleamed brighter and its hilt warmed under her hand.

Alba fidgeted and shook her mane. *Bad thing comes.*

A dark cloud came rolling across the moor. Rhianna stared at it uneasily. The wind blew her hair across her eyes, and she heard large wing beats. Her neck prickled.

Sir Agravaine cursed under his breath. "I hope that's not what I think it is—"

The cloud reached them, swallowing the stones. Sir Agravaine wheeled his horse and readied his lance. Alba gave a frightened whinny. Everything was a blur of rain and shadows. Then a huge, black-winged monster dived at them out of the storm, trailing blue mist.

"I HAVE FOUND YOU, PENDRAGON!"

It was the shadrake that had attacked them last year. She'd banished it to Annwn at least twice, but it seemed to have a short memory.

Rhianna drew Excalibur. But Sir Agravaine lowered his lance and charged past her. "Leave the creature to me, damsel! Go and warn the others. I doubt it's alone."

She knew she should do what Sir Agravaine said, and fetch some of the men back around the spiral to help. But they wouldn't be much use against a dragon, let alone one from Annwn. She raised Excalibur to see better. Dragon and knight were battling in a confusion of black wings and rain turned to sleet by the creature's icy breath.

As she hesitated there was a shriek, and something small and feathered arrowed out of the storm towards her. Alba whinnied in alarm and *misted*.

Somehow, Rhianna managed to stay in the saddle. Then she recognised the little falcon and laughed in relief. "Merlin!" she gasped as the bird darted up into the cloud again.

"I'll take care of this, Rhianna Pendragon," called the druid. "Stay there." The bird disappeared into the cloud.

She heard a crash and grunt of pain as the shadrake swooped at the knight again. Sir Agravaine's horse came galloping towards them, riderless and wild-eyed. She squinted through the rain, and her heart sank. Shadowy figures armed with axes were running down from the Wall and leaping across the ditch. In a few moments they would reach the fallen knight.

She made a decision. "Tell that stupid horse to follow us," she told Alba.

She got the Pendragon shield over her arm and did up the straps with her teeth. Then she urged the mare out of the circle towards the fallen knight. Sir Agravaine's loose mount followed them obediently.

The merlin and the shadrake were still performing a strange sky dance, the dragon chasing the little bird, while the merlin darted out of range and swerved among the stones to escape. Lines of frosty heather appeared across the moor as the shadrake breathed ice after it. Each time it missed the merlin, it had to flap clumsily to change direction. Then it hit a wing on a stone and rolled over.

That dragon will never catch him! Alba snorted. *He is too fast. He says we are to keep clear.*

Finally, Rhianna saw what was happening. Merlin was luring the shadrake towards the approaching bloodbeards, who saw the creature flying straight at them and fled back again to take cover in the ditch.

Sir Agravaine stumbled to his feet and ran to his horse. He gave Rhianna a furious look. "What are you still doing here?"

"Saving your life!" Rhianna yelled back.

The merlin circled and returned to the stones with the shadrake still on its tail. She hastily raised her shield, but the creature did not attack.

"GIVE ME THE DARK EYE, PENDRAGON," it said.

Rhianna frowned. For a moment, she couldn't think what the dragon meant. Then she remembered the mirror, which Arianrhod had taken with her in the wagon. She laughed. "I haven't got it any more. If you want it, you'll have to come to Camelot. Now go!"

"THAT CAN BE ARRANGED," the shadrake said, swooping up into the cloud.

As the creature flapped off, the merlin landed on her wrist. His feathers were ruffled and his little heart beating fast.

"Time you weren't here, Rhianna Pendragon," he panted. "Quickly now, let me get this path closed before any of those bloodbeards sneak through. I've had a little trouble with that half-brained shadrake since I saw you last, or I'd have been here sooner. Move, girl, and get that mist horse of yours back to Camelot. You can do no more here."

"Is Mordred out there, too?" Rhianna craned her neck, trying to see past the stones. The bloodbeards were still cowering in the ditch. "We might be able to get the Lance of Truth back..."

"Don't even think about it," Sir Agravaine growled.

"Go!" The merlin pecked her wrist. "I'll fly back the long way. I don't fancy getting trapped in the spiral path again, and I want to see what that dragon's up to. Try not to get into any more mischief before I get back."

Rhianna hesitated a moment longer. But if Mordred had come with his men, he was keeping out of sight. She sheathed Excalibur and sent Alba galloping after Sir Agravaine. Taking off again into the storm, the druid drew the path closed behind him in a shower of sparkling feathers and vanished.

By the time they reached the other end of the spiral path, nearly everyone had gone on ahead to Camelot with the queen and Sir Lancelot. The sun was shining, just as Sir Bedivere had promised. A flattened area of grass showed where Arthur's pavilion had stood for their picnic, and crushed flowers scented the air. So long ago it seemed, yet it had only been a few days. She wondered what the other squires and damsels had thought when they woke up to find them gone.

Alba snorted in relief and lowered her head to nibble at the grass. *Tastes stale*, she said, spitting out the squashed stalks in disgust. Then a horse whinnied, and the mare pricked her white ears. *Evenstar is here!*

Rhianna felt almost too tired to raise her head as Elphin came running to take her rein. He saw the blood on her wrist and gazed anxiously into her face, his eyes violet with concern.

"*Faha'ruh*, Elphin," she said wearily. "I'm all

right – it was only the merlin's claws. He came back like he said he would, only—"

"*Faha'ruh*, Rhia," he said, putting a finger on her lips. "I thought I'd lost you."

She managed a grin for her friend as she slid to the ground and into his arms. "Not that easily, you don't."

"What happened? The knights who came through last said something about a dragon."

"The bloodbeards turned up with the shadrake."

Elphin's eyes darkened. "Then I hope it ate them!"

"It had a good try. Merlin stayed behind to see what it's up to. I hope he doesn't get hurt."

Sir Agravaine coughed, and they broke apart, remembering they weren't alone. Elphin was still looking at her with those violet eyes full of Avalonian magic. Rhianna flushed.

Cai and Arianrhod came running across to join them with Sir Bedivere close behind, demanding to know what had happened. She explained about Merlin's trick and the dragon chasing the bloodbeards into the ditch. Agravaine muttered something about it being a good thing it had, or they'd both be dead by now. Elphin relaxed slightly.

"Yah!" Cai said. "Serves them right. We showed 'em, didn't we, Damsel Rhianna?"

"We lost the Lance of Truth," Rhianna reminded them. "Mordred took it."

"Well, it'll be a while before he dares bring his army south," Sir Bedivere said. "So let's get back to Camelot before everyone thinks I got their princess murdered on a picnic, shall we?"

"Good idea," Sir Agravaine grunted. "Better

sneak her in the back way, though, before her mother sees her. Just look at the state of you, Damsel Rhianna!"

Embarrassed, Rhianna smoothed her hair. "What's wrong with me?" she said.

Sir Bedivere was fighting a smile. "Where's that mirror gone? Show the girl what she looks like."

Arianrhod pulled out the black mirror and held it up so she could see herself. Alba snorted at it, and Rhianna stiffened.

She eyed the glass warily, but it reflected back only her own face. She saw a cloud of frizzy red hair with the sun in it and smudges on her cheeks. At least her freckles had faded with all that northern rain. She scowled as she remounted Alba. "Well? What do you expect? I just need a bath, that's all."

Everyone laughed. She grinned too. But she looked at the mirror thoughtfully. Mordred's mother had said it was a spirit channel, and it had belonged to her cousin. As they rode back to Camelot, a daring plan began to form.

The Dark Knight Accepts a Challenge

Mordred leaned on the Lance of Truth and glowered about the room that should have held his prisoner. When it became obvious that they couldn't stop his cousin and her friends escaping through the stones, he'd left his men to deal with the stupid dragon and ridden straight back to the tower. The last thing he'd expected to see, when he'd dragged himself up the stairs, was an open door and an empty bed.

He snatched up the end of the chain and frowned at it. The links still sparkled faintly.

"You fools!" He flung the chain at the useless bloodbeards he'd left to guard the queen. They ducked as it clanged off the wall. "Are you trying to tell me you let a damsel and a fairy with a harp break my mother's enchantments and steal my hostage from a locked room? What were you doing while they were cutting her free? Picking your filthy noses?"

"They used m-magic on us, Master," stammered one of the men cowering by the door. "And the damsel had a sword…"

"Of course she had a sword! I know Excalibur's work when I see it." Mordred clenched his fist. "So my cousin's not only stolen my mirror, she's spirited her mother away through those druid stones, too!

This goes from bad to worse."

"B-but you have the m-magic lance, Master."

"Yes I have, and don't you forget it!" He gripped the bedpost so he could swing the lance at the guard, who paled and stumbled backwards down the stairs. His friend grabbed him just in time to stop him breaking his neck.

Mordred smiled. He supposed that, on the whole, a magic lance was slightly more use than his mirror. At least he could use it as a crutch when he was out of his saddle. The queen had served her purpose.

He sat on the bed to rest his crippled leg.

"M-master?" asked the nervous guard. "What should we do now? Do you want us to go south after them?"

He frowned. "Not yet. They'll be back at

Camelot by now. Go help bury the dead, and leave me in peace. I need to think."

The men went, shoving each other in their eagerness to escape.

Mordred lay back on the bed and closed his eyes. For the first time in his life, he couldn't ask his mother what to do. She'd always been there to help him – first in the flesh, and then in the mirror. But she'd messed things up for him, sending that stupid dragon to take care of Merlin last winter and giving the druid's spirit an escape route. And she hadn't been a lot of use at the duel, come to think of it, letting his cousin and her fairy friend get past her spells and bring the knights inside the fort.

"I don't need you, Mother," he muttered. "If it hadn't been for you, I might have the Sword of Light and my cousin in here now—"

"*Mordred*," said a voice.

He sat up with a jerk. The lance was glowing faintly where he had propped it against the bedpost. His spine prickled as the air in front of him darkened, forming a circle the size of his stolen mirror. The circle sparkled faintly around the edges, and a face looked out at him... magic.

He broke into a sweat, afraid his mother had found a way to send her spirit from Annwn to punish him for what he'd just said. Then he realised that the face had freckles and was framed by red hair, and his stomach jolted in recognition.

"Cousin?" he said warily.

The green eyes focused on him. She smiled. "Yes, it's me. Were you expecting someone else? I found this mirror at the fort when you were busy duelling. Careless, leaving a magic mirror lying around like that."

He scowled at her, annoyed that she'd found out how to use the magic, but curious too. "What do you want?"

"I want the Lance of Truth you stole from Sir Lancelot, of course. And I know you still want the Sword of Light. How about we finish the duel? Winner takes both Lights."

Mordred sat up straighter, interested now. "I want my mirror back as well."

"Agreed – but only if you win. If you lose, I'll smash it."

He winced. "Where can we tilt?"

"There's a lake near the battlefield where you fought my father. Do you know it?"

His mind raced. Too close to Camelot. It would be dangerous. They might be planning some fairy magic. His mother would no doubt advise against it, but the witch had lost touch with the world of men. Her methods had failed. Now it was up to him to put things right.

"Tilt against a damsel?" he said, curling his lip. Surely she wasn't stupid enough to ride against him herself? He held his breath in hope.

"No." She frowned. "You'll meet the Pendragon's champion, of course. Strict rules this time."

"I thought Lancelot was dying."

"Your poison failed. Elphin's healing him."

Mordred frowned. He'd beaten Lancelot back at the fort, but that had been with his mother's help. In his Uncle Arthur's day, no challenger had ever bested the Pendragon's champion in a fair tilt. But this time *he* would have the magic lance, and Lancelot couldn't use the Sword of Light, even if the crazy girl let him borrow it.

"When?" he asked, still wary.

She hesitated, and he smiled to himself. So the great knight could not be fully healed yet.

"Midsummer's Day," she said in the end.

Mordred made a swift calculation. That would give him time to round up his rabble and get them into position. His lip curled. Strict rules for the duel, maybe. But he'd have a backup plan in place.

He smiled again, feeling sure of himself for the first time since he'd killed King Arthur. "I'll be there," he promised.

◄❮ 10 ❯►

Queen Guinevere

At the Table Round a queen did call
For her knights to march to Mordred's hall,
While her champion dying of poison lay
And a damsel named the reckoning day.

"Meeting of the Round Table! Queen Guinevere's orders!"

The herald's voice, echoing in the courtyard below her window, woke Rhianna from a confused dream of dark mists. For a heartbeat, she couldn't remember where she was. She could still see that tower room north of the Wall, with its broken chain and crumpled bed, where her mother had been held prisoner. Then the sunshine streaming into her room reminded her that she was back at Camelot.

She smiled. *Queen Guinevere's orders.* They might have lost the Lance of Truth. But her mother was safe, and Camelot had a queen again.

She pushed back the covers, and something clattered to the floor. Her eye fell on the mirror she'd used to contact Mordred before she went to sleep, and her smile tightened. It hadn't been a dream, then. She had really challenged her cousin, and he was coming to finish the duel with Sir Lancelot at midsummer.

She climbed out of bed with a groan, quickly picked up the mirror and hid it under her pillow. She dared not look into the glass again. Her entire body ached. Her left hand had blisters from swinging Excalibur in the bloodbeard camp. She opened her clothing chest and dragged out her favourite green dress, shouting for Arianrhod.

The girl came at once, smiling brightly.

"It's a lovely day, my lady!" she said. "Camelot knows the queen is back."

"Never mind the weather… I'm going to be late for the meeting! Why didn't you wake me?"

She'd meant to get up early and catch her mother at breakfast, but using the witch's mirror had made her sleep more heavily than she'd expected. She strapped Excalibur, back in its good red scabbard, around her waist over the dress. It looked a bit strange, but the knights had grown used to her wearing it like that.

She hurried down the stairs with Arianrhod chasing after her, trying to brush her hair.

"Queen Guinevere said to let you sleep, Rhia. She said they'd be discussing a lot of boring things, and you could join them later. Elphin came to wake you earlier, but Lady Isabel wouldn't let him into the Damsel Tower." She giggled. "I'm sure she thinks he'll charm us all away to Avalon with his fairy harp if she does. So he said he'd go down to the stables and give your mist horses a bath. They got very dirty in the north."

Rhianna pushed the brush away. "Stop that. My mother said to let me sleep? Are you sure?"

"Pretty sure. She told me herself." Arianrhod smiled again. "She also said if I let you appear at the meeting with your hair in knots and wearing your sweaty armour, she'd chain me in the dungeons. So *please* can you let me brush it?"

Rhianna sighed and let her friend untangle the knots she'd made in her sleep. Her hair had grown over the winter and was almost back to its old Avalonian length. It frizzed in a copper cloud after last night's bath. She smoothed her dress and straightened the scabbard. "Better?" she asked, raising her chin.

Arianrhod giggled. "You look like you usually do, only cleaner."

"That'll have to do, then. Go and tell Elphin where I am." She marched up to the big double doors of the Great Hall, put her hands on her hips and glared at the guards until they let her in.

"Rhianna Pendragon!" they announced.

The queen looked her up and down and

frowned at her frizzy hair. The knights nearest the door turned to grin at her. Rhianna did not smile back.

As usual when she stepped into that vast hall, she felt dizzy. The hole above the centre of the table showed a circle of bright blue sky. A sparrow fluttered around the rafters, twittering, reminding her of Merlin the last time they'd met in here. She thought guiltily of her challenge and hoped he'd managed to give the dragon the slip.

She hesitated. All the seats were taken except two – one near the door, where she'd seen her cousin Mordred's shadow sitting on her first night at Camelot, and the other at the far side of the hall, next to the queen. She walked slowly around the huge table to give the dizziness time to pass. She smiled at her mother and started to slide into the vacant chair.

"No!" The queen put her hand in the way. "This is Lancelot's seat."

The knights stopped talking and looked at them. Sir Bors cleared his throat. "With respect, Majesty, that's where Damsel Rhianna usually sits."

Guinevere gave him a fierce glare. "I am your queen. *I* say where people sit at my husband's table, not you."

A hush fell. Rhianna frowned. She didn't want an argument with her mother on their first morning at Camelot, especially not in front of all the knights. But neither did she want to sit in Mordred's old seat. The very thought made her shudder, and obviously nobody else wanted to sit there, either.

"Sir Lancelot won't be here this morning," she pointed out. "So why can't I sit there until he's better? After all, this is a round table, so it doesn't really matter where we sit… does it, Mother?" She smiled sweetly at the queen.

The knights chuckled.

"The princess is right, Majesty," Sir Bedivere said, clearing his throat. "I'm sure King Arthur would say the same if he were here."

Guinevere blinked. For a moment, she looked as if she might cry. Then she took a deep breath and lifted her hand.

Rhianna slipped into the chair, feeling unexpectedly shy. At previous meetings, with the knights arguing and thumping the table around her, she hadn't minded speaking up. Today, sitting beside her mother, she felt like a little girl. She clenched her fist on Excalibur's hilt for strength. Somehow, she had to persuade the knights that getting the lance back was important, without letting them know about her challenge. Otherwise, they might try to stop the dark knight coming to the lake.

As she wondered how much to tell them, Sir Bors thumped his big fist down on the table, making her jump. "Right, let's get back to business, shall we? We've got to decide what we're going to do about Mordred. He kidnapped our queen and held her to ransom, which ain't right. He also nearly killed Lancelot, but that was in a duel so not strictly against the law—"

"Mordred cheated!" Guinevere said. "You told me he used magic in that fort. How can my poor Lancelot be expected to fight against magic? And Mordred's blade was poisoned. That's against the rules, too. I demand you take an army north directly and teach the witch's brat a lesson." She lifted her right hand to show them the red mark around her wrist. Her eyes flashed. "Look what he did to me! He kept me, your queen, in chains all winter… and you're saying he didn't act against the law?"

Rhianna frowned.

Sir Bedivere cleared his throat. "Prince Mordred must of course be punished for the way he treated you, Majesty. But it's as well to be cautious. We might have destroyed his army and made peace with the Saxons down here. But we've seen with our own eyes that he's still got quite a rabble up there behind his Wall. With Lancelot sick, and King Arthur dead… er, I mean *sleeping* in Avalon… we don't have a leader." He glanced at Rhianna. "The time is not right for revenge."

"And don't forget Mordred has the Lance of Truth now," Rhianna said.

Guinevere gave her a distracted look. "That old thing doesn't work any more, Rhianna darling. It's not important."

"I think it is… Elphin mended it using his harp before the duel so Lancelot could defeat Mordred."

"Well, that proves it's still broken, because Lancelot lost the tilt," Sir Bors said.

The knights whispered among themselves, arguing about fairy magic.

The queen frowned. "It's true what Bors says. Forget the lance. Those silly Lights of Merlin's have done us all a lot more harm than good, if you ask me. Half Arthur's knights lost their lives chasing after the Grail, and Arthur himself died with Excalibur in his hand.

I've been informed the Crown of Dreams is missing, thank God. And now Merlin seems to be missing, too. So we'll have to do this the Roman way, by strength of arms. Have we got enough men to take on Mordred's rabble in the north, if Cynric's Saxons ride with us?"

The knights glanced at one another uneasily.

"Maybe…" Sir Bedivere began.

"Don't forget the Saxons fought with Mordred against Arthur," Sir Agravaine said with a scowl. "They've changed sides at least three times already. You can't trust them in a battle."

"They might follow the damsel," someone suggested.

Rhianna's heart beat faster. She hadn't thought the knights might decide to ride north again so soon. That would ruin everything.

But Sir Bors shook his head. "Damsel Rhianna's goin' nowhere near that Wall!" he said firmly. "Not after what happened last time."

And Guinevere frowned and said, "My daughter can't lead an army. Don't be so silly."

Rhianna opened her mouth to say she had already led an army last year during the battle for Camelot, when she'd made peace with the Saxons they planned to use as allies in their fight against Mordred. But she didn't want them suddenly deciding to take her north again, not now. So she bit the words off and said, "Mordred might come here."

"He wouldn't dare," Sir Agravaine growled. "He knows we'd whip his behind halfway to Annwn for laying hands on our queen!"

"Hand," one of Lancelot's men corrected. "Arthur chopped off his other one at Camlann, and I noticed he ain't got it back yet." A few of the knights chuckled.

Sir Bedivere smiled and said, "He hasn't got enough men to take Camelot, anyway. Our little jaunt up at the North Wall let us see that much, at least."

"But what if he thinks the Lance of Truth makes him invincible? He might come then, mightn't he?" Rhianna insisted, unable to believe that the knights could joke about such things.

"Ha!" Sir Bors grunted. "If he does, then he's even stupider than I thought! We'll thrash the little traitor black and blue, an' chain him up in the dungeon where he belongs."

The queen rubbed her sore wrist and nodded.

Sir Agravaine shook his head. "Bedivere's right. He won't show his face south of the Wall this summer. We should use the good weather to strengthen our defences and ride out to recruit more men. Then we can train 'em up over the winter, and maybe next spring we'll have enough of an army without the Saxons to march north and root out Mordred, once and for all. No sense in losing half our men because we're badly prepared. Lancelot ought to be better by then, too. I hear the fairy prince is healing him with his magic harp."

The knights nodded and started arguing about which villages could spare men and horses, how many troops they'd need, and who would ride in which direction.

"But you can't leave Camelot unprotected!" Rhianna stood on her chair so her voice would carry and rested Excalibur, point down, on the table before her.

The knights who had been in the north with Lancelot the last time the Round Table had met frowned. The others looked at her warily, remembering the way she'd used the sword to open the spirit channel and show them their queen in chains.

The queen put a hand on her arm and hissed, "Get down, Rhianna dear. You're embarrassing me."

Rhianna shook her mother off. "I know my cousin," she said. "He'll come this summer, I know he will. You should keep the men together at Camelot in case they're needed, not send them riding all over the country on some silly recruitment mission! Mordred might only have one hand now, but he can still fight with it, and if the Lance of Truth is working again—"

"Which it isn't, darling. I already told you that." Her mother gave her an exasperated look. "I don't know what Lord Avallach's people taught you in Avalon, but it's clear they didn't teach you many manners… standing on chairs, whatever next? Sit down and be quiet, there's a good girl, and let those of us who know what we're talking about decide what to do about Mordred. You've only met him once. We know him a bit better than you do. He's always hidden behind his mother's skirts. Now Morgan's dead and can no longer protect him, he's not going to do anything that involves risking his cowardly neck, believe me."

Rhianna wanted to tell her about all the spirit journeys when she'd met Mordred last year, and how she'd spoken to Morgan Le Fay's spirit in Annwn using the mirror. But it would take too long to explain, and she didn't really know how the spirit magic worked, anyway.

Some of the knights seemed to think Queen Guinevere was right, and the lance was still broken. Others – the ones who had seen Elphin's magic at work up by the North Wall – weren't so sure. The argument went on and on. She bit her lip, wishing Merlin would fly back through the hole in the roof and tell them all how stupid they were being.

She stepped on to the table and gripped the hilt of her sword, meaning to *make* them listen. Then someone coughed softly behind her, and she turned to see her father's ghost sitting in the chair she had vacated. One of his legs rested casually over its carved arm, and a scarred hand played with Guinevere's hair. He looked up at Rhianna, an amused glint in his blue eyes.

"*I know what you did, daughter*," he said. "*Do not worry. I will help you. Remember, Lancelot knows the truth about the lance.*"

Rhianna held her breath. Could the others hear him, too? The last thing she wanted was them guessing her plan.

But the knights and the queen carried on arguing, not even noticing that she had yet to sit down. Her father's ghost winked at her as it faded from sight, and she had an idea how to delay them.

She clenched her fist on Excalibur's hilt and said loudly, "You want to know what I learned in Avalon, Mother? Magic! I saw it working around me every single day, and Merlin says the four Lights are the most powerful magic of all. Mordred used magic at the North Wall, and he'll use it again if he can. You can't leave Camelot unprotected until we find out if the lance is mended or not. Sir Lancelot will be able to tell us when he's better. At least wait until then before you send the men away."

That would give her a chance to tell the champion knight about the duel.

"What are you doing up there still?" her mother said, frowning at her. "If you've got something to say, sit down and say it like a civilised person."

But Sir Bors grunted. "The damsel's right. Caution's our best bet for now. We need to speak to Lancelot before we go up against Mordred, any rate. We'll keep the men at Camelot till he's well enough to answer questions, discuss it again then."

The others nodded. They seemed relieved

that someone had made a decision.

"Lancelot might still die," Sir Agravaine muttered darkly as Rhianna jumped down from the table.

Thankfully, the queen did not hear. She touched her hair where King Arthur's ghostly hand had rested and smoothed Rhianna's skirts. "I'll be sending some clothes and jewels up to your room," she said. "When we meet again, I don't want to see you wearing that sword. It's not suitable attire for a princess of Camelot."

Rhianna started to ask how she was supposed to have rescued her mother from Mordred's tower without Excalibur. But the queen said, "Not now, darling. Lancelot needs me," and hurried from the hall.

⚜

Rhianna almost ran after her. But the thought of watching her mother stroking Sir Lancelot's hair while the champion knight lay in an enchanted sleep was too much. So she headed for the stables.

The warm smell of the horses calmed her. Alba's coat shone in the shadows, and her mane fluffed in a silver cloud. Rhianna let herself into the stall and flung her arms around her mare's sweetly scented neck.

Where have you been? the little horse asked. *Evenstar's rider made me wet! I almost dissolved.*

"Oh beautiful one, I'm sorry… I had to see my mother, but she cares more for Sir Lancelot than she does for me!" Anger filled her. "I was the one who rescued her, not Sir Lancelot! He lost the duel. Without me, he'd be dead."

Alba bent her head to sniff her. *Why are you upset? You are not hurt. I am not hurt. Your mother is not hurt. We won the race, didn't we?*

Rhianna had to smile. "Yes, my darling," she said, finding a brush and setting to work on the mare's mane. "We won, and my mother's safe. But things aren't quite as simple here as they are in Avalon. You might have to race the black stallion again…"

"That mare is clean enough, Rhia," an amused voice said from the passage. "I bathed her for you. What kept you?"

She whirled. Elphin was stroking Evenstar's nose. She wondered how long he had been standing there.

"Elphin!" she said in relief. "Didn't Arianrhod tell you? I had to go to a meeting of the Round Table. How's Sir Lancelot?

The knights said you've been playing your harp for him."

"All night and most of the morning." Elphin came to lean on the barrier. He shook his extra fingers and grimaced. "The magic is not easy outside Avalon, but Lancelot's spirit is strong."

Her heart leaped. "Is he better now, then?"

"Not yet. He needs more healing songs, but the queen told me to leave."

"She didn't want me in there, either." Rhianna pulled a face, and Elphin touched her cheek where an angry tear had escaped. She wiped it away, embarrassed. "It doesn't matter. She's bound to be upset about Sir Lancelot. I think she really loves him. How long do you think it'll be before he can fight again?"

Elphin shook his head. "I don't know, Rhia. Poison's a difficult thing to heal. He won't die, but he'll be very weak for a while."

"Will he be better by midsummer?"

The violet eyes studied her. "Why? What's happening at midsummer?"

She hesitated. Those eyes, full of the light of Avalon, held hers. She could never keep a secret from her friend. Besides, she needed his help. She glanced round to check that there were no squires listening, and told him what she'd done.

Elphin's eyes darkened to purple. "You challenged Mordred to another duel? Are you crazy, Rhia?"

"Maybe… it was all I could think of to get the lance back. So can you heal Sir Lancelot by then? He doesn't have to be fully recovered, only strong enough to sit on his horse and look the part. The main thing is to get Mordred to come to the lake so we can make him give us the Lance of Truth."

"And exactly how are you planning to do that?"

Two squires ran down the corridor. One had a bucket of water, which he threw over the other boy, making him yell. The horses tossed their heads and whinnied. *Stupid human boys*, Alba snorted. *Now that poor horse will go thirsty.*

Elphin joined her in the mare's stall and pulled her into the shadows at the back. They were whispering now. "Because if you're planning on duelling with him yourself, you can forget it right now."

The thought had crossed Rhianna's mind. But only as a last resort, if Lancelot was not better in time and the knights refused to help her.

She grinned. "I'm not that crazy. I've got Mordred's mirror now, so he can't use magic to cheat again. You can use your harp to help Sir Lancelot, like you helped Cai when he tilted against Gareth, can't you? And when it's too late to stop the duel, I'll warn the knights so they can trap him at the lake. Mordred will be a long way from home this time, so he can't just gallop off again to hide behind his wall."

"He won't come alone," Elphin warned.

She nodded. "I know. But when we've got the Lance of Truth back, we'll have two of the Lights, and he'll have none. The knights should be able to overpower him easily." She hoped so, anyway. "The important thing is can you heal Sir Lancelot in time?"

Her friend sighed. "I'll try my best. But I think we're going to need more than my harp if we're going to catch the dark knight. Any sign of Merlin yet?"

"Not yet." Rhianna frowned, remembering how the druid had warned her not to get up to any mischief before he got back. "He wouldn't be much use anyway – he'd probably fly off after another rabbit or something. That's why I picked the lake. I'm going to ask Lady Nimue to help us."

Elphin looked thoughtful. "The lake spirit will want something in return, and you can't give her Excalibur again."

Rhianna smiled. "Of course not! Don't worry, I'll think of something else she might like."

Healing

Harp and love did heal the knight
And made him strong enough to fight,
But no enchantment in the land
Could wrest the lance from Mordred's hand.

Now that the queen had returned to Camelot, all the damsels wore their best dresses and spent ages doing each other's hair in the latest styles. Determined to turn Rhianna into a real princess, Guinevere kept her promise made at the Round Table. Every day an excited

Arianrhod brought new dresses, new jewellery, new sandals, or a new tiara to tame her hair.

Rhianna ignored the dresses and took the jewels to the lake, hoping to lure Nimue, the fish-lady who had given her Excalibur the previous year, out of the water so she could ask for her help with Mordred. But there was no sign of the Lady of the Lake. And when Rhianna swam into the depths to look for the underwater cave where Lady Nimue had tested her with riddles to see if she was worthy to carry the Sword of Light, she could no longer find it. She briefly considered offering her the magic mirror instead. But if it was a thing of Annwn, like Elphin said, Nimue might be angry and then refuse to help them.

Every time she failed to contact the Lady of the Lake, she returned to Camelot in a bad mood. She knew she should tell the champion knight about the challenge, but she could never catch him alone. The queen was with him every waking hour. She wanted to ask Merlin's advice, but weeks slipped past with no sign of the silly bird. Elphin said his druid soul must have turned feral, and they shouldn't count on his help. At least Sir Lancelot's fever had broken thanks to her friend's healing music.

Three days before the duel, knowing she could delay no longer, she marched to Sir Lancelot's room.

The guards at the door smiled at her and called her their 'brave princess'. Rhianna managed a smile back and talked them into letting her in.

To her relief, the champion knight was sitting up, looking much better. Her mother sat on the end of his bed, pouring him water and trying to make him eat something. They had been laughing softly together when the door opened, but fell silent when Rhianna barged in.

"My daughter!" the queen said proudly. "I could hardly believe it when she came to rescue me. Would you ever have believed she'd grow up to be such a fierce warrior?"

Sir Lancelot examined her with his pale eyes. "She certainly took me by surprise when we first met," he grunted, rubbing his throat in memory. He got out of bed stiffly and bent his knee to Rhianna. "It seems I owe you my thanks, Princess. Both for rescuing my queen, and for saving my life in that duel. I might have known Mordred wouldn't stick to Arthur's rules."

Rhianna felt a bit embarrassed. "Oh, get up," she said. "You only got wounded because you charged off to that silly duel without waiting for me to tell you what Merlin said. You might have beaten Mordred if you'd listened to me."

Her mother's eyebrow rose. She looked at Sir Lancelot. "Would you have done?"

The knight frowned as he sat beside her on the bed. "Maybe. There was dark magic at work in that fort. It distracted me, and I dropped the Lance of Truth. The fairy prince tried his best, but it's obviously not working properly. Your mother tells me the knights want to talk to me about that… as good a reason as any for staying in bed!" He grinned, then sobered again. "Mordred had no intention of letting me out of that fort alive, however the duel went. If I'd have killed him, and Damsel Rhianna here hadn't broken the enchantment, I've no doubt his bloodbeards would have sent my soul to Annwn by now."

The queen gave a shudder and crossed herself. "God forbid."

"But I'm alive," Lancelot said, taking her hand. "Mordred might have stolen the Lance of Truth, but he can't use its magic. I'm still the Pendragon's champion until there's a new king on the throne of Camelot."

"Or a new queen," Rhianna said.

Lancelot gave her a thoughtful look. "Perhaps," he said. "But Bors tells me Arthur's going to return from Avalon soon to lead us again. Is that true?"

Rhianna sighed, still trying to think how to tell him about the duel. "Maybe... I don't know. I haven't blooded Excalibur, so I can still take it back to Avalon for him. But his body is not healing as well as it should, which is why I need to find the other three Lights. Mordred's got the Lance now, the Crown's still missing, and the Grail—"

Sir Lancelot gave a harsh laugh. "The Grail? Forget it, Princess! That thing's already killed half Arthur's best knights. If Merlin brought you out of Avalon in search of it, then he deserves everything that's happened to him. I hear he's still stuck in the body of a bird? Good! Maybe we'll all get a break from his crazy plan to set Arthur up as some shining saviour of the world. Arthur was a man, just like the rest of us, as Mordred proved at Camlann – the little traitor." He spat on the floor. "I should have killed the ungrateful wretch in that fort, and to Annwn with the rules! Probably won't get another chance now."

Rhianna bit her lip. She glanced at her mother, whose hand was stroking Lancelot's hair again. "I need to talk to you, sir."

"Go on then," Lancelot said with a smile. "I'm listening."

"I mean alone."

They exchanged an amused look.

"I'm your mother, Rhianna darling," Guinevere said. "Anything you have to say to Lancelot can be said in front of me."

Rhianna met her gaze. "This can't. It's Pendragon business."

Sir Lancelot whispered something to the queen. She frowned at Rhianna, but got up and left the room. The knight glanced at the open door. "Let's take a walk," he said. "These walls have ears."

Rhianna looked at his wound doubtfully.

She could see fresh blood on the bandage.

Lancelot grinned and put an arm across her shoulders. "Good as new!" he said, getting up with a wince. "Your friend's magic is a lot better than old Merlin's used to be."

They headed for the rose garden. Last time Rhianna had been here, white winter roses had bloomed in the snow. Now it was a mass of scented pink flowers, twisting around pillars and rambling up the walls of the castle. Birds sang among the leaves, unseen.

Lancelot led her to the fountain and perched on the rim. "Right," he said, checking that they could not be overheard. "So what's the great secret?"

Now she finally had the champion knight's attention, she didn't know how to say it.

"Mordred's coming to finish the duel,"

she blurted out. "You have to be at Nimue's lake at midday on Midsummer's Day to meet him."

The champion knight blinked at her then burst out laughing. "I'm to kill the dark knight in three days' time?"

"Well… not exactly kill him…" She explained the plan.

"I can see why you didn't want your mother to hear that!" Lancelot said. He got up from the fountain and paced around under the roses. "You're even crazier than everyone says you are, if you think I'm going to be strong enough to fight in three days!"

"It'll be strict rules this time, and I'll tell the other knights what's happening in time for them to get up there and help you. So as long as the lance's magic doesn't work for Mordred, you should be all right," Rhianna rushed on, thinking he might be scared.

"I should be all right? By that I suppose you mean not actually dead?" He shook his head at her in disbelief. Then he sighed and said, "It would be good to get the lance back from Mordred, I suppose – might give me a chance to skewer the traitor."

"There's something else," Rhianna said. "Something important Merlin told me. He said you have to use the lance in the right way. With the right things in your heart. Merlin says that's why it broke when you jousted against my father, and I think that's why it didn't work for you when you tried to use it against Mordred. I'm not sure how the magic works, but if your heart is true when Mordred tries to use the lance against you, maybe you'll win this time?"

Sir Lancelot frowned at her. He pressed a hand to his wound. "You dare suggest my heart isn't true?" His voice was dangerous.

"I know you fought my father over the queen." Rhianna took a deep breath. "But what were you thinking when you met Mordred at the fort?"

"What business is it of yours?" he growled. "I'll have quite enough explaining to do to the knights without you interrogating me, too! Why didn't you tell me about this challenge of yours earlier? I've been lying in bed under your fairy friend's enchantments dreaming of Avalon, when I should have been out training... Of course, Mordred probably won't come, but we'd better be prepared if he does, and I'm certainly not riding up to that lake alone so he can kill me with my own lance. Stay out of things you don't understand, Princess!" He started back towards the castle.

She called after him, "You're the Pendragon's champion! If you won't do it my way, then I'll have to joust against him myself!"

Her voice echoed around the walls. Servants, hurrying along the colonnade beside the garden, looked round curiously. Lancelot stopped, his shoulders stiff, and turned to glower at her. "If you were a squire, I'd whip your cheeky behind halfway back to Avalon," he growled.

"But I'm not a squire, am I?" Rhianna smiled sweetly at him.

"Unfortunately. You've got more guts than half of them." The knight sighed. He came back and said more quietly, "I was thinking of your mother, of course. I care for her. You must know that by now. I doubt the gossip at Camelot's stopped any since I've been away."

Rhianna nodded. "I know that. But why did you want to rescue her?"

"Why? Because I love her! What other reason is there? But why did you risk *your* life to rescue her? Tell me that. There's no love lost between you two, I've heard. It's no surprise, really. You were still a baby when Merlin took you to Avalon. You barely knew her."

"Because she's my mother and I want her to be safe. I'm not sure if I love her though. I can't really remember her, except in my dreams." Rhianna took a deep breath. "I wanted to rescue her for my father's sake, and for Camelot, so things can be right again in the world of men."

"For King Arthur and Camelot…" Lancelot sighed. His hand rested briefly on her shoulder.

"Maybe I have lost sight of what's important. All right, Rhianna Pendragon, you've made your point. When Mordred and I meet at the lake, I'll bear it in mind."

"Not in your mind... in your heart!" Rhianna called after him as he staggered back inside.

Sir Lancelot merely raised a hand without looking round. She noted that his other hand was pressed to his wound, and felt a bit guilty about asking him to duel with the dark knight again so soon. He might be killed this time, which would distress her mother. But he was the Pendragon's champion. Camelot needed him.

❊

Happy at Sir Lancelot's recovery, Queen Guinevere announced a feast at midsummer to make up for the joust that had been interrupted by the dead rider bringing Mordred's grisly message. The next two days were a whirl of preparations as the cooks baked pies and the damsels decorated the halls with flowers. People from the neighbouring towns and villages came to celebrate the queen's safe return, and the camp on the river meadows grew until Rhianna could hardly sleep for the noise.

In a way, the holiday was a good thing because everyone would be at Camelot, which meant Mordred's bloodbeards couldn't slaughter them on their way to the duel. But then Arianrhod told her the queen wanted to present her to the people at the feast as the official heir to the throne, and Rhianna's heart sank.

She couldn't be in two places at once. What if someone came looking for her at the lake?

Her wet hair had not gone unnoticed, and word had got around that she went swimming there. The last thing she needed was for someone to stumble up there early and alert Mordred to the trap. She would have to talk to her mother.

The day before midsummer, she hid Excalibur under the straw in Alba's stable and told the mist horse to call her if anybody tried to touch it. Then she headed for the royal dining hall, where the queen ate now that Lancelot was up and about. It meant wearing a dress and embroidered slippers instead of her more comfortable tunic and leggings, but it was the only place to catch her mother sitting down.

By the time she arrived, Guinevere's plate held only crumbs and the queen was discussing last-minute arrangements for the feast with Lady Isabel.

"Mother?" Rhianna said. "I have to talk to you. It's important."

The queen smiled at her. "Ah, Rhianna darling! Just the person I want to see. Now, remember we're going to present you to the people at the feast tomorrow as Arthur's heir. I want you to look like a real princess, so you'd better start getting ready about midday. Arianrhod will help you bathe and do your hair. You can wear your new dress – the crimson one with the gold ribbons – and that pretty ruby tiara I sent you. We'll soon find you a suitable suitor now you seem to be turning into a young lady at last."

Rhianna bit her lip. The ruby tiara was the first offering she'd made to the Lady of the Lake.

"But that's what I wanted to talk to you

about. I might not be here at midday…"

"Don't be silly, darling. Of course you will. Where else will you be? Off in the woods with your fairy friend? You've got to grow up sometime, you know."

"But—"

"Not now, darling." Her mother rose in a rustle of skirts and gave Rhianna a peck on the cheek. "I've got a hundred and one things to do."

As she left the hall, she glanced back at Rhianna and whispered something to Lady Isabel. They both laughed.

Flushing, Rhianna snatched an apple from the bowl and made her way to the stables.

She'd hoped Sir Lancelot might be there so she could check he was ready for tomorrow, but she couldn't see his white stallion. Alba whinnied to her, smelling the apple.

"My mother cares more about stupid jewels and feasts than she does about me," she told the mare, as they shared the apple. "And now she wants to marry me off! She obviously never expects my father to return... and Lancelot's vanished somewhere, too. It'll serve everyone right if I joust against the dark knight myself!"

You are upset again, said the mare with a little snort. *Do you want to find Evenstar's rider?*

Elphin. She'd forgotten to check his blisters had healed enough for him to play his harp to help Lancelot tomorrow at the duel. She looked over the stall to see if her friend was with his mist horse. The stable was empty.

"Where's Evenstar?" she said, her heart pounding uneasily.

They go to the warm lake that has sweet grass, with the pale knight.

She didn't have to ask which lake. Her mare had grazed there while she'd dived for Excalibur last winter.

"But it's too early!" Her heart jumped. "Why would they go there now? It's not midsummer until tomorrow…"

Then she knew. "Mordred! He's tricked us, hasn't he? He's come a day early!"

She grabbed Alba's bridle and looked down at her dress and slippers with a grimace. It was already past midday. No time now to run up to her room and change. She rummaged under the straw for Excalibur. Good thing she hadn't left her sword in her room, too. She'd just have to do without her armour and hope Mordred had not killed Lancelot before she got there.

Not stopping for a saddle, she led the mare out into the sunshine, hitched up her skirt and vaulted on bareback.

"Where are you going, Damsel Rhianna?" Cai called from Sandy's stable.

"Tell the knights to come to the lake!" she called back. Before anyone could stop her, she was galloping through the gates and across the bridge.

12

A New Champion

Terrible was the duel that day
When Mordred journeyed south to slay,
Upon the shore of an enchanted lake
Champions fought for a damsel's sake.

Alba was fresh after standing in her stable. She kicked up her heels, eager to find Evenstar. Rhianna lost her slippers at the first buck, but did not stop to pick them up. She let the mare gallop as fast as she wanted, not caring when the breeze tugged her hair from its pins and tangled it with Alba's sweetly scented mane.

They took the fastest route along the Roman road then galloped over the surface of the river in a sparkling spray. Alba's hooves, shod with Avalonian silver, did not even get wet. Rhianna grinned as she remembered how the sight of her mist horse galloping alongside their boats had astonished the Saxons last year. Today there were no boats, just a confusion of hoofprints in the mud on the other side. The distant clash of weapons came from the wood, sending a shiver down her spine.

She crouched lower over the mare's neck as they entered the trees, swerving dangerously around the trunks and ducking branches. She didn't see the bloodbeards in the shadows until Alba reared in fright. They had dragged a fallen tree across the path and were standing on it, watching the duel.

"Halt!" called one of the men, spinning around at the sound of Alba's whinny. "This is private business."

"Let me through!" Rhianna snapped.

The man relaxed slightly, jumped down and fingered her dress. "Well well, what have we here?" he said. "A damsel out riding, all alone in the big bad woods?" The others chuckled as he peered behind her. "Where's your escort, lassie?"

"I don't need an escort," Rhianna said. "Not when I've got *this*!" She drew Excalibur and swung the blade at his mocking grin.

"That's no ordinary damsel," one of the men warned as he ducked in alarm. "That's the Pendragon girl!"

The others scrambled for their weapons.

But they were too slow. Alba had already jumped the barrier and was misting through the trees. Rhianna heard hooves pounding after them and shouts from the men, and kept her head down.

"Faster, Alba!" she said.

Water sparkled silver through the leaves ahead of them. She saw Evenstar standing under the trees, his white coat streaked with sweat and his saddle empty. As she looked anxiously for Elphin, the little horse rolled his eyes and snorted at Alba.

He says the men fight in the water. The stallions make big splash. He is frightened of the shining spear.

Rhianna gripped Excalibur tighter, staring across the lake. The shining spear… she didn't like the sound of that.

Sir Lancelot's white stallion and Mordred's black galloped towards each other along the beach, kicking up a glittering spray. Rainbows glimmered around the Lance of Truth, which was strapped to Mordred's crippled arm. Sir Lancelot had his lance tucked under his arm, too, but it did not shine like Mordred's. The champion knight hunched over his horse's neck, and she saw blood on its white coat.

Elphin crouched on a rock just off shore with his harp. His fingers danced across the strings as the two knights met. The light brightened around them until Rhianna could not see what was happening. "Remember – in your heart!" she shouted to Sir Lancelot. The champion knight glanced her way, distracted. At the same time, a small brown pony burst out of the woods with Cai clinging on bareback, barged past Alba and galloped straight for the two horses.

"No, Cai!" she shouted, hoping he had remembered to give the knights her message.

Sir Lancelot yelled a warning. Elphin's harp sang louder. Rhianna raised Excalibur and urged Alba after the squire – too late.

She heard a great CRASH and a grunt of pain. There was a whirl of legs and arms. Then Mordred's horse came galloping out of the water, its bridle hanging half off. The dark knight was still in the saddle, but he had dropped the lance. The dangling reins had got caught around his crippled foot. He was trying to untangle them with his remaining hand. His stallion shook its head in anger, flattened its ears and charged at Alba.

The mare misted again, and Rhianna almost

fell off. She grabbed Mordred's bridle to stop his horse attacking hers, still trying to see what had happened to Cai.

The white stallion pulled up at the end of the beach, where the champion knight slid slowly to the ground and lay still. She felt a bit sick. What if he was dead? What if Cai was dead? Then the spray cleared, and she saw the Lance of Truth glimmering on the beach halfway along the shore.

"I'll get it!" yelled Cai. The boy had already jumped off his pony and was picking the lance out of the mud. She let out her breath in relief.

The dark knight abandoned his efforts to free his foot and snatched his horse's reins from Rhianna's hands. He pulled off his helm so he could see better to sort out the bridle, then noticed her dress and laughed.

"I nearly didn't recognise you, cousin! You didn't have to get all dressed up for me, you know. That lance is useless. I might as well have tilted against Lancelot with a squire's spear! But I see you've brought me Excalibur. Saves me the bother of riding to Camelot to claim it."

"You're a day early!" Rhianna said, flushing at his look. "You broke the rules. And now Lancelot's unhorsed, so you'd better not be thinking of finishing the duel on horseback."

Mordred glanced at the fallen knight and smirked. "I'd say your champion is in no state to continue the fight. That leaves you with a bit of a problem, doesn't it? I don't see anyone else here to defend your honour, which means I've won... unless you care to finish the duel yourself?" His eyes glinted a challenge.

"I'm not afraid to fight you with *this*."

Rhianna showed him Excalibur. The white jewel, sensing the magic of the lake, shone brightly.

Mordred looked warily at her sword.

"You should be afraid. I killed your father while he held that sword, remember? I can kill you just as easily."

"Let me fight him for you, Damsel Rhianna!" Cai called.

"How fitting," the dark knight mocked, sneering at the lance in Cai's grip as its head wobbled on the new shaft. "A squire's spear in a squire's hands… careful, Camelot brat, you might hurt yourself."

Cai scowled. "Shut it, traitor, or I'll skewer you with this thing."

Mordred laughed. "Like to see you try."

He renewed his efforts to untangle himself. Rhianna tensed. She opened her mouth to tell

Cai to get the lance to safety. Then Elphin shouted, "Look out, Rhia!" and she saw the bloodbeards running out of the trees to help their prince. The men she'd encountered had been joined by others – they must have the lake surrounded.

She did the only thing she could think of. Before Mordred could straighten, she slid on to the black horse's hindquarters behind the dark knight and put Excalibur across his throat. "Nobody moves!" she ordered.

The bloodbeards stopped warily, eyeing her blade in dismay. Alba snorted uneasily at her. Mordred, who seemed taken completely by surprise, sat up slowly and pressed back against her.

"Well, this is nice," he drawled. "I didn't know you cared, cousin."

"Shut up," Rhianna hissed. "Or I'll kill you, I swear."

Gentle music drifted across the water, and she realised Elphin was playing his harp again. A few of the bloodbeards yawned, but the sleeping magic didn't seem to work very well on them from that distance.

Mordred laughed. "Oh yes, go on, Rhianna Pendragon. Blood your magic blade. Do it, I dare you! Then you'll never be able to take that sword back to Avalon for your dear father, will you?"

"I told you last year, I don't care any more about blooding it. It's not going to heal him, anyway, not on its own. I need the lance as well… Cai," she said, trying to keep both her voice and her sword steady, "take the Lance of Truth to Sir Lancelot, and see if you can get him back on his horse. Nobody else moves, or I'll kill your prince! I mean it."

Cai scowled at the bloodbeards, who stepped back reluctantly. Leading Sandy, he carefully carried the lance along the shore to where the white stallion stood faithfully beside the fallen knight.

Cai bent over Sir Lancelot. He glanced up at Rhianna and shook his head.

Mordred relaxed slightly as her blade lowered. "See?" he said. "Your champion's finished. If he dies, I've won. According to the rules, that means you have to give me the Sword of Light, and I get to keep all Lancelot's possessions. That includes the Lance of Truth, his horse, and his squire, I believe. I'll soon thrash some manners into the little brat, teach him not to interrupt people's duels."

He waved a hand, and his bloodbeards ran towards Cai and Sir Lancelot.

"Tell them to stop!" Rhianna pressed Excalibur harder against Mordred's neck.

"You won't do it, cousin." He laughed at her again. "You couldn't do it last year, and you can't do it now. For all your tough words, you're just a damsel in a dress…"

Her hand tightened on the hilt. She closed her eyes. *Cut his throat. Just cut his throat and have done with it*, she thought. And yet it didn't seem right, not like this.

"RHIA!" Elphin warned.

She'd hesitated too long. The bloodbeard captain, who must have been creeping up behind her while Mordred taunted her, seized her ankle. At the same time, Mordred swung his elbow backwards and knocked her off his horse. She hit the ground in a daze. When she sat up, Mordred had drawn his sword and was galloping towards Cai and Sir Lancelot. The black stallion's hooves sprayed her with grit.

Alba sniffed her anxiously. *Is it another race?*

Rhianna had no breath to reply. The bloodbeard drew his blade and rushed her. She swung Excalibur to catch his blows, desperately trying to remember what Sir Bors had taught her in the training ring. But fighting in a dress was not easy. The long skirt tangled in her legs, and the stones on the beach hurt her bare feet. Further along the shore, guarding the injured Sir Lancelot, Cai gripped his wobbly lance and bravely faced the dark knight and the bloodbeards closing on him.

"Damsel Rhianna!" he yelled, his voice small and far away. "What do we do now?"

What indeed? She must have been crazy to think she could outwit the dark knight, when her father and Sir Lancelot had both failed to defeat him. But she tightened her jaw and danced around her opponent, determined not to let her cousin get hold of Excalibur, whatever happened.

Out of the corner of her eye, she saw Mordred's stallion overtake his running bloodbeards and gallop straight for Cai, intent on trampling the boy.

"*Cai*!" she shouted. But the squire seemed frozen to the spot.

The bloodbeard captain came at her again with his sword. She swung Excalibur in a glittering arc and sent a silent plea for help to the ninety-nine knights whose spirits were linked to the white jewel.

But, distracted by her friend's danger, she couldn't concentrate well enough to wake the magic in her sword. Some of the strength left her arm, and Excalibur lowered. The bloodbeard captain grinned at her. "Getting tired, Princess?" he taunted. "No dragon to help you this time, I see. Can't control the creature, can you. And you've left your brave knights behind. Some Pendragon you are."

She cast a desperate look at Elphin. His harp rippled louder, making the silver light dance over the water. Excalibur gleamed brighter. There was a sudden flash of light from the other end of the beach. She heard a splash.

The bloodbeard looked round and cursed. "The little fool! He's only gone and thrown it into the lake."

She risked a look round, too. Cai no longer

had the Lance of the Truth. Far out in the lake, rainbow ripples spread from where it had entered the water.

Mordred's stallion had spooked at the flash of light. The black horse was galloping away into the trees, riderless, leaving his master in a tangled heap on the ground. The dark knight sat up and pointed at the squire in fury. "Someone kill the little brat and catch my horse!"

The bloodbeard captain left Rhianna and hurried to help his prince. Cai valiantly drew his little dagger as the other bloodbeards prepared to rush him.

Rhianna closed her hand around Excalibur's jewel. "*Please,*" she whispered to the knights' spirits. "*Please, come.*"

Sparks of colour fizzed out of the lake where the lance had sunk beneath the surface.

Evenstar and Alba pricked their ears and stared at the water, nostrils flaring. The air above the lake filled with rainbows, and a sweet scent drifted across to the shore. Elphin's harp fell silent. His eyes lit up with the fabulous colours. Even the bloodbeards hesitated, staring at that rainbow light.

There was an eerie hush.

Then a troop of ghostly knights rode out of the rainbows and came cantering silently along the shore, led by King Arthur riding his golden mare.

"*Father!*" Rhianna's heart leaped in hope. He looked so solid. Could two of the Lights be enough to restore his soul to his body? Maybe Merlin was wrong, and she didn't have to take the Sword of Light back to Avalon for him, after all? Maybe throwing the lance into the lake was enough, and he had come back to the world of men to reclaim his throne?

Mordred stared at the king and the knights in disbelief as they cantered closer. There was still no sound, just that sweet scent and the rainbow light and the glowing horses bearing down upon the dark knight. Mordred staggered to his feet and stood swaying in their path. Then his nerve broke, and he stumbled towards the trees. The bloodbeards turned tail and fled after their prince, chased by the ghostly knights.

They are stupid, Alba snorted. *They think those knights are alive.*

Rhianna shook herself. Of course, it was only her father's ghost again. King Arthur's body still slept in Avalon's crystal caverns, and those knights were dead. She felt faintly disappointed, but still warm inside. Her father hadn't forgotten her.

Sir Lancelot was sitting up now, blinking in confusion after the ghosts. Cai ran to help him. She sheathed Excalibur with a grim smile. Keeping half an eye on that rainbow shimmer where the lance had entered the water, she vaulted back on to her mare and cantered across to Elphin's rock.

"Ride Alba back to shore," she said. "I'll dive down and try to find the lance."

Elphin shook his head at her. "You're crazy, Rhia, taking on Mordred like that… I thought he was going to kill you! You're not even wearing your armour."

"Just as well. I can't swim in my armour." She was already tying up her skirt. "Here, hold Excalibur for me. I don't want that fish-lady getting hold of my sword again."

"I'm not sure the lady of this lake likes being called a fish," Elphin said carefully, staring past her. Rainbows reflected in his eyes and he gripped his harp tighter.

Rhianna turned, a shiver going down her spine.

The fish-lady who had given her Excalibur last year was perched on a nearby rock with her strong tail curled around it. She wore the tiara Rhianna had thrown into the lake first of all, the rubies glowing like fire in her green hair. The Lance of Truth rested across her glittering scales, gripped firmly in her webbed hands.

"You seem to have a habit of offering me gifts and then trying to take them back again, Rhianna Pendragon," she said.

"Lady Nimue," she breathed. "You came!"

Turquoise eyes regarded them in amusement. "Why so surprised? I heard you when you called me before. But I have no use for these trinkets." She pulled off the tiara and cast it back to the shore, where Cai picked it up. His eyes widened as he stared at the fish-lady. "This, however…" She stroked the lance. "This is a powerful weapon, almost as powerful as Excalibur. It is a suitable offering in return for my help, I think."

"I'm very sorry, Lady Nimue," Rhianna said. "But Cai made a mistake."

Nimue laughed. "Like that knight made a mistake offering Excalibur to me last year, after Mordred killed King Arthur?"

"Er… yes. But this is different. Sir Lancelot isn't going to die."

The fish-lady looked at the beach and

nodded. "You're right. He won't die now he has given up the Lance of Truth."

What did she mean by that? Rhianna eyed the glimmering lance and looked impatiently at the trees. "Please can I have it back, Lady Nimue? Mordred's getting away."

Nimue shook her green hair. "Do not be too greedy, Rhianna Pendragon. You already have the Sword of Light. If you want this lance, then you must answer a riddle."

Rhianna scowled. "I answered your riddles last time!" She kept an eye on the trees. It wouldn't take Mordred and his bloodbeards very long to realise that they were running from ghosts, and then they'd be back.

Nimue smiled. "Not all of them, I seem to remember. I asked you, 'Who carries the Lance of Truth?' Last time, you said 'a knight', and I let you get away with it."

"Well, I was right, wasn't I?" Rhianna said, growing impatient. "Sir Lancelot is a knight!"

"Before I give you the Lance of Truth, I'll need to know a name."

Rhianna sighed. "Sir Lancelot, of course," she said, looking doubtfully at the wounded knight. What if he wasn't strong enough to carry a lance any more? Was that what the fish-lady meant?

Lady Nimue shook her head. "Its magic no longer works for Sir Lancelot. He carried it once for his king, and he broke it. You need to find someone else to be your champion now."

"Elphin mended it with his harp…"

"The Avalonian prince did his best. But this lance was made by the hands of men, and its magic will only work for one whose heart is true. So who carries the Lance of Truth? Come on, it's not a trick question. He's already carried it once. When a knight cannot fight, his squire must take up his arms."

Rhianna followed the fish-lady's gaze to the shore, puzzled, and saw Cai standing guard over Sir Lancelot with his dagger.

Lady Nimue laughed her tinkling laugh. "I think your new champion's going to need a better weapon than that little dagger if he's going to defend your honour against the dark knight," she said. "Don't you agree, Rhianna Pendragon?"

She stared at Cai, realising at last what Nimue meant. She started to laugh, then looked at Cai's determined jaw and smiled. It seemed the only way they would get the Lance of Truth back. "Cai?" she called. "How would you like to be my champion?"

"I already am your champion, Damsel Rhianna!" Cai called back, not understanding.

"I mean my proper champion, who answers all challenges issued against the Pendragon and fights on my behalf when I ask you to, as Sir Lancelot fought for my father and the queen."

Elphin's eyes whirled violet. "Merlin's not going to like this," he said.

Sir Lancelot frowned. "I don't think—"

"Cai carries the Lance of Truth!" she shouted. Before the injured knight could say another word, she trotted Alba across the water, snatched the lance from Nimue's webbed hands and carried it to the beach. "Go on, Cai," she said, holding the lance out to the gaping squire. "Take it."

Sir Lancelot shook his head. "Oh no, Princess… you don't understand what you're asking! The boy'll never manage a full-sized lance. For all our sakes, choose another lad. He's not even a knight. The Pendragon can't have a common squire as a champion."

"Is that so?" Getting impatient, Rhianna thrust the lance point down into the sand and dismounted. "Kneel, Cai," she ordered.

Cai cast a nervous look at Sir Lancelot, then knelt obediently before her and bowed his head. She brought Excalibur down flat on the boy's shoulder – first the left, then the right. The white jewel blazed. Cai gasped as the light surrounded him and faded back into the blade. Rhianna's hand tingled strangely.

"Arise, Sir Cai," she said. "Now get back on your pony and pick up that lance!"

The boy flushed and, with a bit of a struggle, remounted Sandy. "I'll train every day until I'm strong enough to carry it, Damsel Rhianna!" he promised, grasping the shaft. As he closed his hand about the lance, its shaft glittered and shortened slightly. Its head gleamed in the sun as it came free of the sand, reflecting in Cai's eyes and turning his hair to gold. Even Sandy's normally dull mane glowed like fire.

Cai looked a bit surprised. Then he balanced the lance one-handed, levelled the point at a tree, and set his heels to his pony's sides. Rainbows glimmered and leaves showered around them. He trotted Sandy back with a plum proudly impaled on the end of the lance, grinned at them all and said, "It's really light! I reckon Sir Lancelot's been havin' us on about it being such a heavy burden to carry all these years." He pulled the plum off the end and ate it.

Rhianna smiled, remembering how lightly Excalibur had sat in her hand when she'd first held the sword in Nimue's underwater cave last winter. She'd only wanted to get the Lance of Truth off the lake spirit and safely back to Camelot. But it seemed she'd done more than simply answer a riddle.

"Its magic is working again," Elphin said. "I thought it must be, when Mordred fell off his horse earlier, but I wasn't sure."

Sir Lancelot looked a bit uneasy. But he couldn't argue with the facts.

Smiling in satisfaction, the fish-lady slipped back into the water. "Good luck with the rest of your quest, Rhianna Pendragon!" she called in her musical voice, as she dived with barely a ripple. "Give my love to Merlin when you see him again."

They watched silently until her glittering tail had vanished into the depths. Elphin sighed, slipped his harp back into its bag and went to soothe Evenstar.

"Right, Damsel Rhianna!" Cai said, holding the Lance of Truth proudly with its shining head pointing at the sky. "Who do you want me to fight?"

Rhianna started to laugh, meaning to tell him to save his energy for Gareth in the squires' tilt. But Sir Lancelot drew his sword and scowled at the trees. "Reckon you can start with that lot," he said quietly.

She saw shadowy figures moving through the wood and remembered Mordred.

THE DARK KNIGHT MEETS AN OLD ALLY

"Come back, you cowards!" Mordred's crippled leg gave out not far from the lake, and the ghostly horses passed him in a rush of light and wind. "King Arthur's dead," he yelled. "I killed him, remember? Those knights are not real – it's just more fairy magic!"

The noise of his bloodbeards fleeing through the undergrowth faded into the distance. The last of the leaves settled, and silence fell. He leaned against a trunk and frowned at the trees. Every way looked

the same. He whistled hopefully for his horse.
But the animal was long gone.

He scowled at his empty right gauntlet.
If he still had both his hands, he would never
have lost the duel or the lance. It had been
that useless squire's fault, getting in the way
when he'd been just about to skewer Lancelot!
And then the boy had thrown the magic lance
into the lake right under the nose of his horse,
spooking the stupid animal. What an idiot.
But at least his cousin didn't have the lance,
either. The bottom of the lake was the best
place for the useless thing.

As his heart steadied he heard men's
voices, twigs cracking underfoot, and the
snort of a pony. He peered warily through the
trees, worried that his cousin had come after
him, and recognised the unmistakeable yellow

braids of his old ally Cynric, the Saxon chief who had fought on his side in the battle against King Arthur.

Mordred smiled and brushed himself off. This could work out better than he'd anticipated. "Cynric!" he called. "Well met."

The Saxons stared at him silently. The big chief looked Mordred up and down, and his face broke into a grin.

"Prince Mordred," he said. "I thought it was your men we saw running through the woods. You're a long way from home."

Mordred scowled. "Camelot's my rightful home, as well you know. The Pendragon throne ought to be mine by now. You owe me a favour, Cynric."

"What do you want?" the Saxon said, hands on his hips.

"I've got a small problem up at the lake. Nothing a few men can't take care of, except my cowardly lot have run off, as you saw. Scared by ghosts, the fools."

Cynric frowned. "Saxons have promised not to fight any more battles for you."

"Won't be much of a battle." Mordred chuckled. "One knight is wounded, and the others are just half-trained youngsters. The rest of Arthur's knights are getting ready for their midsummer feast at Camelot, probably drunk already. But we have to be quick in case help turns up."

Cynric smiled. "Is that so?"

The Saxon was getting irritating. Mordred eyed the pony, but it was already laden with furs, and he didn't fancy riding a scruffy Saxon pony when he met his cousin again. "Are you going to help me or not?"

"You're in luck. We're going that way." The chief nodded to his men. "Help Prince Mordred, then. He seems to be having trouble walking these days."

Two burly Saxons gripped Mordred's elbows. Their hands were rough, and he growled at them. But they were strong and solid, unlikely to spook at ghosts. He leaned on them in relief as they escorted him back to the lake.

◄◙ 13 ◙►

Saxon Gifts

Gifts of furs did the Saxons bring
To welcome home the wife of their king,
And a prisoner bound for the traitor's cell
When under the squire's lance he fell.

At first Rhianna thought the bloodbeards had come back, and dropped her hand to Excalibur's hilt. Then a broad-shouldered man with yellow braids stepped out of the trees, draped in dark furs despite the heat. A golden torque gleamed around his throat. With relief, she recognised Chief Cynric, who had laid siege to Camelot last winter but later surrendered to her after losing the battle. Other long-haired Saxons stood behind him, their spears glittering.

"Sneaky barbarians must've crept up on us while we were talking to the lake spirit," Sir Lancelot muttered. He gathered up his stallion's reins and made a valiant attempt to get back into the saddle, but failed. He groaned and pressed a hand to his wound, fresh blood on his fingers.

Rhianna smiled. In the rush to rescue her mother, obviously nobody had thought to tell Sir Lancelot about the peace treaty she'd made last year with the Saxons.

Then Cynric beckoned to his men. Two burly warriors stepped out of the trees supporting a figure in muddy black armour between them.

Her stomach lurched. "*Mordred*!"

Thinking of what Sir Agravaine had said about the Saxons having changed sides three times already, she drew Excalibur. Cai levelled the Lance of Truth at the chief and warned, "Don't come any closer!"

Sir Lancelot gave up trying to mount, and twisted his free hand into his horse's mane instead. "Stay close to me, Damsel Rhianna," he said quietly. "You too, fairy boy – any magic you can manage that'll get us out of this wood in one piece will help. Cai, don't you dare drop that lance! They're on foot. Once we're clear of these trees, you should be able to lose them on the road to Camelot. I'll delay them as long as I can…"

"Do you need any help, Pendragon Princess?" the Saxon chief called. "We were on our way to the celebrations, when we spotted this one's bloodbeards running through the wood. Then we found Prince Mordred lurking in the bushes and heard your voice. Thought you might be in trouble." He frowned at Lancelot's wound. "Did they attack you?"

Rhianna relaxed. The hands on Mordred's arms seemed to be restraining him rather than supporting him. "It's all right," she told her friends. "Chief Cynric doesn't fight for Mordred any more. The treaty still holds." She sheathed her sword and started forward to greet the Saxon.

Sir Lancelot grabbed her rein and pulled her back. "*What* treaty? Last time I met these Saxons was on the battlefield with my king, and that man fought under Prince Mordred's eagle! You can't trust a barbarian – they change sides faster than the wind. You'd make a nice little hostage for them, I'm thinking. Don't be fooled by how things look. You know how sneaky the traitor is. A poisoned blade and turning up a day early for our duel is nothing compared with what the dark knight is capable of!"

She hesitated. What if he was right, and her cousin had rejoined his old allies? The Saxons outnumbered them at least five to one, even without Mordred's bloodbeards. Lancelot's wound hadn't healed properly yet, and Cai had not had any practice with the Lance of Truth.

"Am I any use to you as a hostage, Chief Cynric?" she called, hoping he wouldn't say 'yes'.

Cynric chuckled. "Only if Prince Mordred's paying," he said, glancing at their prisoner. "But he seems to have come down in the world since I saw him last. We found him skulking in the woods like a beggar without horse or weapon. You're the one with the gold round these parts, Pendragon Princess. Besides, if we break the treaty, Arthur's knights would be down upon our villages like a flash, scaring our wives and children. The last thing we want is their horses' clumsy hooves trampling our crops when we've only just planted them. I prefer to take a few furs to the queen and drink her mead at this big feast she's promised us all tomorrow. Going to see you all dressed up and named as Arthur's heir, I hear? That'll be something to sing about."

Rhianna grimaced at the reminder.

"And him?" Sir Lancelot said, pointing his sword at the glowering Mordred. "You really think we're going to let you into Camelot with the traitor who killed King Arthur?"

Cynric shrugged and glanced at the dark

knight. "We can just as easily slit his throat here and dump the body in the lake, if you like. He's no use to us. But we thought you might like to execute him with a bit more ceremony, considering he killed your king."

"Let me go, you barbarian scum!" Mordred scowled at the chief and heaved against his captors. "You agreed to fight for me if I got rid of King Arthur! I kept my side of the bargain. I thought you were supposed to be helping me." But, crippled and unhorsed, he didn't have much chance of escaping his Saxon captors, who pushed him to his knees.

Rhianna frowned. If it was a trick, her cousin was playing his part well.

"Good idea," Cai said, keeping the Lance of Truth levelled at the dark knight. "Cut the dirty sneak's throat."

Mordred paled as one of his captors caught hold of his hair and dragged his head back.

"No!" Rhianna said, seeing Cynric reach for his dagger. Uneasily, she remembered her cousin pressed against her with her blade across his throat. She frowned at Cai. "Not like this... Mordred might have killed my father and kidnapped my mother, but he's got Pendragon blood, same as me. He should be taken back to Camelot so he can be tried properly for his crimes."

Cynric looked a bit disappointed, but slipped his dagger back into its sheath.

"Well said, Damsel Rhianna," Sir Lancelot agreed. "And when my wound's properly healed, maybe we'll get a chance to finish our duel."

"I'm the Pendragon's champion now,"

Cai reminded them. "I should finish it."

Nobody took any notice of the squire. They were all watching the dark knight, who kicked and cursed as the Saxons bound his elbows behind him.

Eventually, Mordred's struggles ceased. He glared at the chief, panting. "Mother warned me never to trust a Saxon!" he spat. "She'll haunt you and your children for the rest of your miserable days, you two-faced barbarian dog."

Cynric laughed. "I'm not afraid of your curses, witch's brat. Gag him, too," he ordered his men. "I'm sure Princess Rhianna doesn't want to hear that kind of language all the way back to Camelot."

Since most of the party were on foot, they took

the short cut over the hills. At first Cynric's men were wary, keeping a lookout for any bloodbeards who might try to rescue their prince. But Mordred's men had vanished, along with his black stallion and the ghostly knights. By the time Camelot's towers came into view, glittering like fire in the setting sun, the Saxons had relaxed. They shoved the prisoner along between them, taunting him about his cowardly troops who had run off to save their own skins.

Sir Lancelot rode at the front beside Chief Cynric, quizzing the Saxon about the new settlements, while the chief rested a hand on the white stallion's rein to keep him steady for the wounded knight. Elphin examined the Lance of Truth curiously, and Cai experimented by carrying it in different positions, poking poor Sandy in the ribs and making Evenstar mist to avoid it.

Rhianna rode at the back to keep an eye on her cousin, who breathed heavily around his gag as the Saxons hauled him along. She couldn't help feeling a bit sorry for him. Yet, if their positions were reversed, she knew he'd have no mercy. She felt uneasy about taking him to Camelot. She wanted to talk to someone who could advise her on what to do next. But her mother would not understand, and she'd more or less given up on Merlin.

"Rhia?" Elphin said, breaking into her thoughts. "Did you tell the queen where you were going?"

She realised they had reached the final track leading up to Camelot. She didn't think her mother would even have noticed her absence, considering how busy she had been with preparations for the feast. But as they came in sight of the walls, the gates opened and a company of knights cantered down the hill to surround them with flashing lances.

"No further!" growled Sir Agravaine, lowering his lance to stop Cynric. He glowered at Mordred. "Damsel Rhianna, Elphin, Cai... take your ponies inside. Everyone else, don't move. That includes you, Lancelot! The queen wants to know what you think you're doing, putting her daughter in danger like this?"

The big chief spread his hands and glanced at Rhianna. Sir Lancelot looked pale, and swayed in his saddle. Rhianna dismounted and opened her mouth to explain. But before she could say a word, Sir Bedivere trotted down to join them, bringing the queen on the hindquarters of his horse. Guinevere slid off the mare and flung her arms around Rhianna, hugging her tightly.

She was so surprised that she closed her mouth again. Her mother's hug was warm and soft, exactly as she had imagined it would feel, all those years she was growing up without her in Avalon. Her eyes pricked with unexpected tears.

She is crying, Alba observed with a surprised snort. *But she is happy also. Humans are very confusing.*

"Thank God you're safe!" Guinevere gasped. "When I heard you'd galloped off bareback without even your armour, I didn't know what to think! The knights came back reporting the woods were full of bloodbeards but could find no sign of you. Then we saw you coming over the hills with the Saxons and

Mordred, and I feared the worst…" She cupped her hands around Rhianna's face and blinked away her tears. "Oh, my darling! Don't you *ever* scare me like that again!"

"Sorry, Rhia," Elphin whispered. "It's my fault the knights couldn't find you. I told Evenstar to mist across our prints to confuse our trail in case those bloodbeards tried to follow us."

She smiled as she explained this to her mother. Nobody could follow a mist horse's trail unless they knew what they were looking for.

By this time, Sir Lancelot had recovered enough to explain about the duel at the lake and how the Saxons had caught Mordred hiding in the woods. Sir Agravaine reluctantly lowered his lance and let Cynric approach the queen. The Saxon went down on one knee and pulled off his golden torque.

"Please accept this with my personal apologies for worrying you, Queen Guinevere," he said. "As you can see, your daughter is safe and well. And I have brought you gifts to celebrate midsummer."

The queen frowned at the gold, distracted. "I don't want your necklace. It's a man's ornament."

"Then please accept these furs and this prisoner as thanks for letting our families settle in your villages." He beckoned to his men, who led forward their pony laden with furs. They dragged the dark knight forward, too, and pushed him to his knees.

The queen merely gave the furs a passing glance. But she glared at Mordred, who scowled back, unable to protest through his gag. "Accepted," she said in a tight little voice.

When the Saxon chief rejoined his men, Guinevere's attention moved to Sir Lancelot, who still sat on his white horse, clutching his wound. The knights coughed and shuffled their feet. Rhianna held her breath. Would her mother hug him, too, with all the Saxons watching?

But the queen rested a hand on his horse's rein and smiled up at him. "Sir Lancelot," she said, her voice back under control. "I'm pleased to see you've captured Prince Mordred. But, as your queen, I order you to get that wound properly treated before you fight any more duels, do you hear me?"

"Yes, my lady," Lancelot said just as formally. "I'm pleased to report that the Lance of Truth's magic is working again and the Pendragon's honour is safe. With two of the Lights at Camelot and Mordred as our prisoner, we have nothing to worry about this summer."

The queen gave the lance in Cai's hand a doubtful look. She shivered as the sun disappeared behind a bank of cloud. "Looks like a storm brewing. Someone take the prisoner to the dungeons, and let's get back inside. Rhianna, come to my chamber tomorrow when you've changed for the feast. I've got something for you."

❈

Everyone went to bed early that night, tired out after all the excitement. Thunder grumbled around the castle. Rhianna lay awake, turning the events at the lake over and over in her head. Had she done the right thing by knighting Cai and sparing Mordred's life? Thinking of her cousin locked in the dungeons below her room only a few flights of stairs away, she drifted into an uneasy dream.

The dark knight dragged his crippled leg up the stairs. She watched in terror, unable to move, as he pushed open her door and limped over to her bed. He looked down at her, then reached across and slid the black mirror from under her pillow.

"Think you're clever, don't you, cousin?" he hissed. "Getting your hands on two of the Lights? They won't do you any good without the Crown of Dreams, you know."

He turned the mirror to face her. It flashed jewel colours into her eyes, and she saw Morgan Le Fay lying on a shadowy bed. The crown from Merlin's song-pictures glittered in the witch's dark hair…

Rhianna woke in a sweat. Lightning lit up her room. For a heartbeat, she thought she saw the dark knight standing over her. But it was just a shadow cast by her father's dragon shield, which Arianrhod had hung on the wall to decorate her room. She shook her head, feeling silly. She hadn't kept the dark mirror under her pillow since she'd used it to contact Mordred. Only a summer storm.

She padded barefoot to the window and stared out into the night. Another flash lit up the sky, and she glimpsed a winged shape flying over the river. Despite the heat she shivered, worried about Merlin. Could birds fly in storms? What if the little falcon had got struck by lightning on its way home? Would Merlin be able to manage the spirit transfer into another body? Last year he'd spirit-ridden the shadrake to make it bring them his druid spiral, but she didn't think he had the strength to control a dragon again. She thought uncomfortably of how she'd challenged the creature to come to Camelot.

It was still very hot. Giving up on sleep, she sat on the edge of her bed with Excalibur across her lap. Slowly and carefully she polished the blade, making sure it was clean of every smudge of dirt. The action calmed her. She slid Excalibur back into its scabbard and put it under her pillow.

Feeling a bit safer, she dozed off again and dreamed of the dragon flapping around the castle walls, trying to get in but failing.

❈

She woke with a start to hear voices arguing

outside her room. She quickly dragged on her Avalonian tunic and leggings, her heart pounding. If Camelot was under attack by dragons, she didn't want to be caught half dressed.

"I'm telling you, you can't go in there! She's still asleep, poor thing. Worn out by that silly duel up at the lake yesterday."

"And I'm tellin' *you*, Damsel Rhianna will want to know her hawk's returned! I'm the Pendragon's champion now, so I'm allowed to wake her up if I need to."

"Don't be silly. You're only a squire."

"I'm not just a squire any more. I'm a knight now – ask Damsel Rhianna!"

"You?" There was a snort of laughter. "Pull the other one!"

Recognising Cai's and Arianrhod's voices, she relaxed.

"It's true. And I carry the magic lance. So are you going to let me in, or do I have to use this thing on you? I've already unhorsed Mordred with it."

Rhianna fought a smile. "Arianrhod!" she called. "Let him in! I'm dressed."

The door burst open, and Cai charged into her room with the Lance of Truth. Arianrhod followed, clinging to his sleeve. "I'm sorry, my lady, but he just barged right in here..."

"It's all right, Arianrhod," Rhianna said, sheathing Excalibur. "Did I hear you say my merlin's back?"

"Must've flown in overnight!" Cai said. "We found it in the courtyard when we went to feed the horses, with its poor little wings spread out and feathers everywhere. I thought it was dead."

Rhianna thought of the winged shape she'd seen over the river during the storm. She frowned at the open door, where some of the girls had gathered in their nightclothes. They peered in at Cai and giggled. She closed the door in their faces.

"Is Merlin's spirit still inside?" she said softly.

"I think so," Cai said. "I took him to his perch and gave him water and something to eat."

"Good." Another rumble of thunder distracted her. She glanced out of the window. The storm clouds were heavy and black, and the first few drops of rain splashed into the courtyard. "He must have just made it before the storm broke."

"Yeah, it's going to be a good one! Kept me awake all night." Cai went eagerly to the window, making Rhianna and Arianrhod duck as he swung the Lance of Truth around.

"You don't have to carry that lance with you everywhere, you know," Arianrhod grumbled. "There's nobody to fight in the Damsel Tower."

"Sorry," Cai said. "But I don't like to leave it lying around, what with Mordred and them Saxons about. Sir Lancelot said to put it somewhere safe, and this is the safest place I could think of…"

Rhianna barely heard. "I'll be in the hawk mews," she said.

Ignoring Arianrhod's protests that she hadn't brushed her hair or had any breakfast, she took Excalibur down to the mews and pulled the little hood off the merlin.

The bird blinked sleepily at her. It looked so tattered and thin, her stomach fluttered.

What if they'd lost the druid's spirit? Who would help her get the Lights back through the mists to her father's body in Avalon then?

"Merlin?" she said, gripping Excalibur's white jewel. "Can you hear me?"

The merlin turned its back on her and stuck its head under its wing.

"*Merlin*!"

The head came out again. "Not so loud, Rhianna Pendragon!" the bird scolded. "I was having a nice dream."

She giggled in relief. "What was it about? Hunting mice? You must have hunted quite a few of them, the time you've taken to get back here. I've been worried."

The bird fluffed its feathers and eyed her. "Druids do not share their dreams. What do you want?"

My father alive again. My mother to love me.
To be a girl in Avalon again with Elphin.

Rhianna sighed. All those seemed impossible right now, so she said, "I need some advice. Mordred's in the dungeon and Cai's got the Lance of Truth—"

Merlin gave her a sharp look. "Yes, Cai told me all about your little escapade up at the lake yesterday. Are you completely mad, child?"

"I didn't know Cai could talk to you!" She frowned, forgetting what she'd been about to say. She hadn't exactly expected the druid to congratulate her on her plan that had almost gone so very wrong. But she'd thought he would at least be pleased they had got the lance back.

"That boy will talk to anything. Ponies, birds, trees, rocks… it's never difficult to find out what's going on when young Cai's around.

And now it seems Camelot has a new champion, the youngest and most inexperienced knight who ever lived."

The merlin cocked its head at her. "If I'd known about your feather-brained scheme to get the Lance of Truth back from Mordred, I'd have returned sooner. I thought you'd be too tired after your trip north to get up to much while I was gone. I should have known better. You're a Pendragon, after all."

Rhianna smiled and gripped Excalibur. "Yes, and don't you forget it. Where have you been, anyway?"

"Dragonland. I had some unfinished business with the shadrake. Then Mordred's bloodbeards came galloping across the border like the Wild Hunt was after them, yelling about some duel by an enchanted lake, King Arthur coming back from the dead with his knights who had died on the Grail Quest, and Mordred being taken prisoner by the Saxons. I got back here as soon as I could. Whatever made you think it would be a good idea to invite the dark knight to Camelot?"

Her flush deepened. "It was all I could think of to get the Lance of Truth off him. My father's not back from the dead, though. I don't think two Lights are enough to heal him. It was just his ghost they saw."

"Hmm, of course. Yet it seems Arthur's getting stronger, so you must have done something right." The merlin sighed and fluffed its feathers again. "So tell me everything, and then maybe we can sort out this mess."

She told him, and he blinked a blue eye at her.

"Oh, child. You're as reckless as Arthur ever was! I didn't know whether to believe Cai's account. That boy's famous for his stories. But it's worse."

"Worse how?" Rhianna frowned. "Mordred's in the dungeon, and we have the Sword of Light and the Lance of the Truth…"

"So you keep saying. But Mordred can't stay here in the castle. It's too dangerous. His witch-mother will find out where he is eventually, and then she'll use him to get to you."

Rhianna thought uneasily of her dream. "Then what should we do?"

The merlin's reply was lost in a crash of thunder. All the hawks turned their hooded heads to the door, listening to the storm. Merlin hopped to the end of his perch and buried his head back under his wing.

"Merlin!" She scowled at the bundle of shivering feathers. "I saw the shadrake last night over the river. Was it chasing you? Do you think it'll find Mordred? What were you doing in Dragonland…?"

"Go away, Rhianna Pendragon," the merlin grumbled from under its feathers. "Stormy weather's very upsetting for birds. I need to think about all of this, and I can hardly remember my name with that racket outside. Go and enjoy your party. Come back tomorrow."

She could get no more out of the bird. She shook her head in frustration. As usual, talking to Merlin had left her with more questions than answers.

Remembering last year, when the shadrake had attacked her mist horse, she hurried through the passage to the stables. Like the hawks, all the horses were restless. Elphin sat cross-legged in a corner of Evenstar's stable, softly playing his harp to soothe them.

"It'll be over soon, my darling," she promised Alba, slipping into the mare's stall and stroking her soft nose. "A bit of thunder can't hurt you."

The mare snorted. *I do not like getting wet. The sky is very bad today.*

"You won't get wet," Rhianna promised. "We're not going out riding today. I've got to be the princess for a little while." She looked over the partition at Elphin. "Do you think we should check on Mordred?"

He stopped playing and his eyes darkened. "No. The guards will keep a good eye on him, don't worry."

"But Merlin said it's dangerous to keep

him here, and last night..." She shook her head, not wanting to remind her friend about the mirror. "Never mind."

Elphin watched her carefully. "All the more reason to stay out of that dungeon! I don't think you should go down there while he's in there, Rhia."

"But what if he escapes?"

Elphin sighed. "He's crippled and alone, underground, behind bars and a locked door, with armed guards posted outside. What do you think he's going to do? Walk through the wall?"

Rhianna thought uneasily of her cousin's shadows last year, but she sighed. "No, you're right. He'd probably throw something at me."

"And that wouldn't be good just before your mother presents you to your people!"

Elphin smiled. "I hope you're not planning on wearing that sweaty old tunic to the feast?"

"No." She pulled a face. "My mother and Arianrhod have been planning my dress ever since they got back! She wants to see me beforehand, so I suppose I'd better start getting ready soon. It's just... I think I saw that shadrake again last night. What if those bloodbeards come back?"

"They won't," Elphin said firmly. "Not in this weather, anyway. And don't let Mordred ruin your day. He's a lot safer locked up in Camelot's dungeon than riding about the land terrorising people with his bloodbeards."

She smiled. Her friend was right about that, at least.

◄◙ 14 ◙►

Summer Feast

Rhianna took the throne that night
To thunderous cheers by lightning bright,
While in dungeon dark and forlorn,
Mordred cursed the day she was born.

Later, soaking in the royal bath, Rhianna remembered her mother's gift and wondered what it would be. She hoped it wouldn't be too embarrassing. There were only two things she really wanted – the two remaining Lights – and as far as she knew the queen didn't have either of them.

As she washed Rhianna's hair with scented oils, Arianrhod told her how worried the queen had been when the knights couldn't find her at the lake. "She was certain you'd either been killed by bloodbeards or drowned, so I told her how you often went out riding in your fairy armour and how good a swimmer you are."

"But I didn't have my armour," Rhianna said.

"I know." Arianrhod giggled. "I told Cai to take it to you, but he was afraid you might throw it into the lake. He'd already followed you up there several times and watched you throw your jewels away." The girl sobered. "Why did you do that, Rhia? Didn't you like them?"

Rhianna pulled a face. "I've got enough

jewels! I can't wear them with my armour, can I? But Lady Nimue didn't want them, either. She was waiting for me to offer her a weapon. I should have realised. I was stupid, inviting Mordred to that duel. He almost killed Sir Lancelot."

"But now Prince Mordred's in the dungeon so he can never hurt any of us again, can he?" Her friend fingered the scar on her cheek and said in a little voice, "Do you think the queen will have him executed?"

"Maybe." Rhianna climbed out of the bath, uncomfortable with the thought.

"She should, after he kept her prisoner in that horrid tower all winter! Is it really true Cai's the Pendragon's champion now?"

"It's true, I'm afraid."

Arianrhod smiled. "He deserves to be.

He's really brave. He'll make a fine knight once he's had a bit more practice. So now Cai carries the Lance of Truth for you. And Elphin's got his harp and the druid spiral so he can do magic for you..." She lowered her eyes. "Maybe one day I'll be able to carry something for you, as well?"

Rhianna gave her friend a sympathetic look. "Of course you will, Arianrhod!" She couldn't think quite what, though. She couldn't exactly imagine Arianrhod fighting a duel for her, and the girl didn't have Avalonian blood so she couldn't learn magic like Elphin and Merlin.

Then she remembered the mirror.

"You can look after Mordred's mirror for me. Elphin says it's a thing of Annwn, but it might be useful. Put it somewhere safe. I'd rather nobody else knows about it for now."

Arianrhod cheered up immediately. "Yes, my lady. I'll polish it for you, shall I?"

"If you like... be careful with it, though." Rhianna held her arms up for her new dress. By the time her friend had finished arranging the long skirts and added the ruby tiara Cai had brought back from the lake, it was nearly dark outside. "I'd better go," she said, worried her mother might dash off again if she was late.

Arianrhod nodded. She finished Rhianna's hair and smiled. "You look lovely, Rhia," she said. "A bath always makes your cheeks glow."

Rhianna thought the less her cheeks glowed, the better. Her freckles were bright enough in summer at the best of times. But she smiled back. "Thank you... go on down to the feast when you're ready. I don't expect I'll be very long, knowing my mother."

She felt rather nervous as she knocked on the queen's door. What if Sir Lancelot was in there, too, and she caught them kissing?

But she needn't have worried. The champion knight was obviously still recovering from his exertions up at the lake. Guinevere opened the door herself, stared at Rhianna in wonder and smiled. For once the queen was alone, without even a maid. Though it wasn't sunset yet, the storm had brought an early dark. The chamber glowed with candles. A fire crackled in the hearth.

"You look beautiful, Rhianna," Guinevere said. She drew her daughter into the room, looked her up and down again, and sighed. "I'm sorry."

"What for?" Rhianna said.

"For avoiding you. And for trying to turn

you into the princess I always wanted you to be. It wasn't until you disappeared yesterday on your little fairy horse, and Sir Bors came back with news of those bloodbeards, I realised... Oh darling, I do love you, you know. It's just that you confuse me! I knew Merlin had brought you out of Avalon, of course. Mordred told me, while he had me captive in that horrid dark tower of his. But I always thought of you as just a little girl. And then you came riding north in your fairy armour with Excalibur shining in your hand and leading a troop of knights like a warrior princess from a song, saying you were going to bring King Arthur back from the dead! I didn't know what to think."

She took a deep breath, walked to the window and stared out at the lightning flickering on the horizon. It was still very warm.

Rhianna wished she'd worn a thinner dress. She waited, not knowing what to say.

Her mother spoke without turning around. "I've seen you looking at us... You have to understand, Lancelot and I are... the truth is we've been in love since we first set eyes on each other, but we promised we would never be completely together until Arthur died. And then after the battle, when we heard the news – well, I'm sure you're old enough to understand. Your father was gone. I didn't want to lose Lancelot as well." She turned from the window, tears in her eyes. "I'm only human, Rhianna. I thought it would be all right if we went to Lancelot's castle in the north, that nobody would mind too much. I should have known Mordred would take advantage of the situation... and then you turned up to rescue me, saying Arthur would be coming back from Avalon soon to reclaim his throne! I blamed you for destroying the happiness Lancelot and I had found together, brief though it was."

Rhianna bit her lip. "And now?" she whispered.

"You mean now Sir Lancelot's back here at Camelot?"

She nodded.

Her mother gave her a steady look. "We won't see each other again, if that's what you want. I'll present you to the people tonight as King Arthur's official heir, and keep the throne for you until you're old enough to marry and your husband becomes king. Lancelot will rejoin the knights and lead them in battle. He tells me he's given up the Lance of Truth, but he's still our best fighter. Then if Arthur returns, he'll find me waiting for him."

She twisted her hands into her skirt and stared out of the window again. The candlelight made her look very young.

Rhianna's heart twisted. But she had to know. "Do you still love my father?"

Guinevere sighed. "I don't know, Rhianna darling. I did once. But we were hardly more than children when we married. What will he be like when he returns from Avalon? Will he be the same age as he was when Mordred killed him? I'm getting older… and so is Lancelot. What if Arthur doesn't come back for years and years? Will he still love me when I'm an old woman? Will he even remember me?"

A shiver went down Rhianna's spine as she remembered what Lord Avallach had said last winter, when he'd tried to take Excalibur back to Avalon so that it would be safe from Mordred. *Arthur will remain with us for many years yet*. She didn't like to think of her mother growing old before he returned. Her father's ghost might be getting stronger now she had two of the Lights, but he was still no closer to being reborn.

"I don't want you to stop seeing Sir Lancelot," Rhianna said with a sigh. "It wouldn't be fair."

Her mother's face lit up. She took Rhianna's hand. "Darling, you're not just saying that because you want me to keep loving you? I'd love you anyway. You're my baby girl… even if you're not quite so much of a baby as I remember you." She gave Rhianna a bemused look. "I know I haven't shown it to you so far, but I'll make up for it, I promise. Just give me a bit of time."

Rhianna bit her lip. "We've probably got lots of time," she admitted. "I don't know how long it'll take to bring my father back from Avalon, but I have to try."

Guinevere smiled. "I know you do, darling. And I'm proud of you. But you really scared me yesterday. You've got to promise me one thing."

Rhianna stiffened. What if her mother made her promise not to go out riding again? How would she ever manage to find the Crown of Dreams and the Grail of Stars if she was stuck inside Camelot? It would be like being back in Lord Avallach's crystal palace in Avalon. Safe, maybe, but boring…

The queen squeezed her hands. "In future, you are absolutely *not* to go out riding without your armour, your shield, your sword, and at least one knight as escort! I also want you to continue training with the squires in the mornings, as Sir Bors tells me you've been doing. Then you can join the damsels at their lessons in the afternoons. That'll set my mind at rest next time you decide to ride on campaign with the knights, but should keep you from turning into a total barbarian in the meantime. Agreed?"

Rhianna couldn't help a grin. "Then you don't mind me going to look for my father's crown when this storm is over?" she said. "A dragon stole it from the battlefield when he died, and I think I might know where it is." She'd been thinking about the crown as she soaked in the bath, and Merlin's detour to Dragonland suddenly made a lot of sense.

The queen frowned. "We'll have to talk about that. I suppose Arthur won't be needing his crown for a while. Which reminds me…"

She reached into her trinket box and brought out a pendant made of a single jewel on a silver chain. The stone looked black in the candle flames, blacker than the sky outside. Her mother touched it with a faraway look in her eye, then fastened it around Rhianna's neck. A crack of thunder made them both jump. "Your father gave me this on the night before his battle against Mordred. It glowed like fire when he kissed me goodbye, but it turned black when he died. I haven't worn it since."

Had her father known he was going to die? Rhianna shivered and fingered the jewel curiously. "Why did it go black?"

"I don't know. But Arthur said if anything happened to him in the battle, I should keep it and give it to you when you were old enough to take the throne."

Her mother stared into the distance again.

The pendant felt strangely cold against her skin. It was heavier than it looked and even uglier than the ruby tiara she'd thrown into the lake. Rhianna couldn't imagine wearing it much. She could always offer it to Nimue later – at least the thing would sink. But she didn't want to upset her mother again, so she smiled and thanked her.

Before she could work up the courage to give her a hug as well, there was a tentative knock at the door. Arianrhod timidly peered into the room.

"Your Majesty?" she said. "I'm sorry to interrupt, but they're ready for you downstairs. The hall is full of people! Sir Bors says you'd better bring Rhianna down, before there's a total riot."

❈

The noise from the feast met them halfway down the stairs... music, laughter, men calling for mead, damsels and squires giggling and shrieking as they chased each other around long tables groaning with food. The hall was alight with candles. Garlands of flowers decorated the rafters and rose petals had been scattered on the floor.

As their queen and their princess entered, a hush fell. People stared at Rhianna in admiration. The younger knights and older squires nudged one another as she passed, and there were a few wolf whistles. She flushed and dropped her hand to where Excalibur usually hung at her belt, but clutched air.

"You look beautiful, daughter," said a voice at her elbow. *"You do not need your sword tonight.*

I will keep the young ones in line."

King Arthur's ghost winked at her and drifted to the back of the hall, where it floated up behind Gareth, one of the wolf whistlers, and tapped him on the shoulder. The squire jumped and looked round, but obviously couldn't see the ghost. Rhianna smiled as the boy stared nervously about the hall.

An avenue opened through the crowd for the queen. Guinevere led Rhianna up to the dais, where two beautifully carved thrones waited with new cushions, and made a short speech about her daughter being of true Pendragon blood and heir to the throne of Camelot. Then she took Rhianna's hand and guided her to the largest throne. As they sat side by side, everybody in the hall went down on one knee and shouted:

"LONG LIVE QUEEN GUINEVERE! LONG LIVE PRINCESS RHIANNA!"

A bard stepped up on the dais and sang about Sir Lancelot's duel with the dark knight. He seemed to have made most of it up. But the people clapped and cheered anyway as the silver-haired champion knelt before the queen. His wound had been freshly bandaged, and he looked much better. Rhianna saw her father's ghost smile, and relaxed. It would be all right, she decided. Sir Lancelot did not want her father's throne. If he made her mother happy, then she was happy too.

Then Cai knelt before her with the Lance of Truth, and was presented as the new Pendragon champion and the youngest knight ever to have a place at the Round Table of Camelot. Gareth scowled and muttered something to his friends, but King Arthur's ghost tapped him on the shoulder again and he shut his mouth quickly.

The queen raised Sir Lancelot, Rhianna raised Cai, and everyone cheered again. They didn't shout for very long, though. The food soon distracted them, and the Hall filled with whirling dancers while the tables jammed with people telling each other wilder and wilder stories of Prince Mordred's defeat.

When her mother went off with Sir Lancelot in search of food, Rhianna sat watching the celebrating people. She knew she should be happy. But she couldn't help remembering that the throne she sat in belonged to her father, while the dark knight who had killed him was still alive in the dungeons below them.

Elphin appeared as if by magic at her elbow, his harp slung over his shoulder. "You look amazing, Rhia," he said, his eyes bright violet as they took in her new dress, the rubies flashing in her hair, and the pendant at her throat. "Is that a new necklace?"

Rhianna blushed. "It's an ugly thing, but Mother gave it to me," she said, turning the black jewel so Elphin could see. "My father gave it to her before his last battle, apparently. She says it used to be a different colour. Is it magic, do you think?"

Elphin touched the jewel with one of his extra fingers. "Maybe. I think it's very old. There's an echo of a song… no, it's gone." He shook his head and frowned.

"I'll ask Merlin about it tomorrow, when he's less grumpy – don't, Elphin! That tickles." His finger lingered on her neck. She playfully slapped his hand away.

Cai pushed his lance between them. "Hands off the Pendragon, or I'll have to challenge you to a duel," he said, and the two jostled each other.

"You dare challenge a prince of Avalon, squire?" Elphin said, teasing.

Cai scowled. "I'm a knight now, remember. And I've got one of the Lights, so you'd better watch out, fairy boy."

"Oh stop it, you two!" Rhianna said, getting embarrassed. "Cai, did *you* tell that bard about Sir Lancelot's duel with Mordred?"

Cai grinned. "Of course! Everyone wanted to know the details. I told him about you attacking Mordred's camp up at the North Wall single-handedly as well, and how we got the Lance of Truth off him, and how you summoned Lady Nimue to help us, and maybe a few other things as well..."

Rhianna groaned. "Oh Cai, you didn't."

Too late. The bard had already taken up his harp again and begun to sing about 'Rhianna Pendragon and the Lance of Truth'.

"He makes me sound like some great hero from a song," she said with a chuckle. "But I couldn't have rescued my mother and got the lance back without you and Arianrhod."

"And we couldn't have done it without you and Excalibur!" Cai grinned. "I just wish I'd been there to see your face when you realised we'd swapped the sword… where's Arianrhod got to, anyway?"

"Oh, she'll be around somewhere. I told her to enjoy herself." Rhianna looked for her friend among the dancers, but a great crash of thunder distracted her. They heard the hiss of rain on the roof.

People looked up nervously. Then the Saxon chief Cynric's big voice boomed out, "It's our god Odin bringing a gift for the Pendragon princess!"

"Well, he can't have her. She's ours!" Cai shook his lance at the roof, and everyone laughed.

While nobody was looking, Elphin leaned over the back of her throne and gave her a light kiss on the cheek. "That's *my* gift until we find your crown," he whispered, driving all thoughts of her dark cousin out of her mind.

Rhianna's skin tingled. King Arthur's ghost raised an eyebrow at her, and she knew she was blushing. Elphin smiled, then took out his harp and jumped down to join the musicians, filling the hall with music until they could no longer hear the storm outside.

In the Dungeon

Far below the dancers in Camelot's dungeon, Mordred sat on a pile of dirty straw, hugging his crippled leg. He peered nervously into the shadows. It was so dark that he couldn't see if anybody else was down here with him. Damp oozed out of the walls. Beyond the bars of his cell, a single smoky torch showed a locked door. Beyond that stood his guards and the stairs the fools had pushed him down. He'd almost broken his neck.

The place reminded him of the cave where he'd spent last winter in darkness and pain, except this time he did not have his mother to talk to. It smelled the same, too – the stink of fear.

"Mother," he whispered. "If you can hear me, just help me get out of here and I'll do whatever you say. I promise. I'll even visit you in Annwn, if you want."

A draught made the torch splutter. He shivered. Where had that wind come from? Camelot's dungeon was sealed tighter than its Damsel Tower.

Pain stabbed up his right arm, and he clutched it with a scowl. It had been hurting ever since that clumsy squire had spooked his horse and made him fall off. The boy would pay, once he got out of here. Champion… ha, what a joke! Mordred scowled in the darkness. With a champion like that, his cousin would not last long on the throne of Camelot.

He heard a scraping at the outer door and stiffened as it creaked slowly open. Had they come for him already? But his guards did not appear. Instead, a slender hooded figure slipped through the crack. He saw something glint under the folds of its cloak and broke into a sweat.

An assassin? Come to slip a quiet knife into his ribs?

The hooded figure paused outside his cell and fumbled a key into the lock.

Mordred scrabbled back into the shadows and clawed his way up the wall until he stood propped against it, heart thudding. He looked around for something to use as a weapon. But his guards had taken anything he might have used before they flung him in here.

"Who are you?" he demanded. "What do you want?"

The mysterious figure did not answer. It opened the cell door and waited in silence. Mordred eyed the shadowy corridor, gathered all his strength and made a stumbling rush for the stairs.

The figure gasped as he knocked it to the floor, and long black hair spilled out from the hood. A girl. Something fell out of her hand, glittering in the torchlight, and a familiar symbol flashed into his eyes – the witch-mark, carved into her pale cheek.

Mordred laughed in relief as he recognised his mother's ex-maid and his stolen mirror. He snatched it up and angled the black glass to the light.

"Mother?" he breathed.

The witch's face appeared immediately. "Don't speak. The guards are taken care of. Your horse awaits you in the courtyard. The side gate is open. The shadrake will lead you to its lair. Get out of here. Now."

Mordred looked down at the still form of the maid. He remembered that she served his cousin now and had been part of the trick with the lookalike sword they'd sent him. He gripped her throat in sudden fury.

"Leave her!" snapped his mother. "She'll be more use to us alive. And leave my mirror so I can reach her – you won't need it any time soon. Go, before the party finishes!"

He did not need telling a third time. He grabbed the torch from its bracket on the wall and dragged himself through the door, past the guards whose throats had been

efficiently cut and up the steps. Thunder
rolled around the castle walls.

At first it was too dark to see anything.
Then lightning flashed, showing him his
bloodbeard captain holding two black horses
in the courtyard. On the battlements, its black
wings spread against the sky, the shadrake was
ripping out the heart of a sentry. Another
dead guard lay near the side gate.

He let the captain help him into his
saddle, then leaned across and whacked him
over the head with the smoking end of his
torch. "That's for letting me get captured, you
idiot! Now get me out of here before I decide
to slit your throat, too."

"Yes, M-master," stammered the
bloodbeard. "Which way?"

"Dragonland, of course! My cousin's got

two of the Lights now. If we don't get hold of the Crown of Dreams before she does, we're in big trouble."

"D-do you know where it is then, Master?" asked the bloodbeard.

Mordred snarled, "Of course I know where it is. And if you don't stop asking stupid questions, you'll be the first to taste its power. GO!"

The man paled. With thunder rolling overhead, they galloped through the open gate and followed the shadrake into the storm.

Available now…

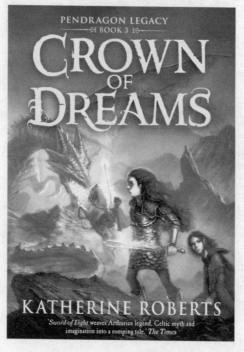

Read on for a preview of Rhianna Pendragon's
third thrilling quest…

Hardback
ISBN 978 1 84877 852 8

THE DRAGON'S LAIR

Mordred reined in his horse and eyed the cave behind the waterfall. A strange green glow came out of it, lighting up the valley. Water dripped from the trees, from his cloak and off the end of his nose. Why did dragons have to make their lairs in a land where it rained all the time?

"So what are you waiting for?" he snapped. "This must be it. Go in there and bring me King Arthur's crown."

His bloodbeards looked at each other uneasily. Seeing Mordred clench his fist, their captain drew his sword and rode reluctantly towards the wall of green water. His horse rolled its eyes and dug in its hooves.

"I think the horses can smell the dr-dragon, Master," he stammered.

"Nonsense!" Mordred said. "The shadrake's forgotten we were supposed to be following it. You all saw it fly off. If it had stuck around, we might have found this godforsaken place sooner."

"Horses sense more than men, Master," the captain pointed out, glancing nervously at the sky.

"Go in on foot, then!" Mordred used his good leg to kick the bloodbeard off his horse. "You can still run if you need to, unlike me. We'll wait out here in case the shadrake comes back."

The captain shuddered. But he knew better than to argue with his master.

Gripping his sword, he vanished into the hillside. Shortly afterwards they heard a muffled yell, followed by the rattle of falling debris. The water glittered eerily green, spooking the horses again. The men paled and crossed themselves.

"Oh, for Annwn's sake!" Mordred snapped. "Do I have to do everything myself? Leave your horses out here and follow me."

His stallion snorted at the water, but stopped playing up when Mordred growled at it. He ducked over the horse's neck to avoid the spray. Its hooves echoed inside the rocky tunnel, which sloped downwards and burrowed deep into the hillside. At every turn, the eerie green glow brightened.

Sweat bathed Mordred as he remembered his underground sickbed, where he'd almost died after his uncle, Arthur Pendragon, wounded him with Excalibur during their final battle. But that had been a whole year ago. King Arthur was dead. The Sword of Light was in the hands of Arthur's daughter, who was afraid to blood the blade in case it stopped her taking the sword back to Avalon, where it would help bring her father back to life. Mordred had no such worries. As soon as he got hold of his uncle's crown, he'd ride to Camelot and blood his blade as many times as was necessary to claim the throne.

They emerged in a vast cavern, which stank of dragon. Jewelled daggers, rusty swords and dented shields were piled around the walls, along with what looked suspiciously like human bones. One of the piles had avalanched, and his bloodbeard captain lay groaning underneath it. His men hurried over to help.

"Leave him," Mordred snapped, seeing that the man was still breathing. "Find the crown, you fools! Quickly, before the shadrake comes back."

While his men searched through the dragon's hoard, Mordred rode his horse slowly around the cavern, prodding at the treasure with his spear. "Where is it, Mother?" he whispered.

"Here, my son," whispered a woman's voice from the shadows.

Mordred froze. His mother's spirit lived in the underworld of Annwn now, and until today he'd always needed her dark mirror to speak to her. "Where?" he said warily.

"Right under your feet, you foolish boy,"

the witch hissed. "What do you think is making the light in here?"

Mordred's horse stopped dead and threw up its head, banging him on the nose. He looked down and sucked in his breath.

His mother's body lay half buried under the treasure, her dress torn and stained. A crown encircled her dark hair, glittering with coloured jewels. As his horse's hooves dislodged the pile, he saw that one of these – a large green stone at her forehead – was glowing eerily. There wasn't a mark on her, and for a wild moment he thought she wasn't dead.

Then he saw her spirit rippling in the green light. *Dark magic.*

His gaze fastened greedily on the crown. He slid clumsily out of his saddle and fell to his knees beside her. He tugged at her dress with his left hand, pushing the dragon's treasure off her body with the stump of his right wrist. "Help me, then!" he yelled at his bloodbeards.

They came running.

"Morgan Le Fay!" the captain breathed, still looking a bit dazed. "So this is where she ended up. I always wondered how she died."

"That dragon must've killed her," said one of the others, looking nervously at the tunnel behind them.

"Don't be stupid," Mordred snapped. "My mother's a powerful enchantress. She controlled the shadrake. It led us here, didn't it?"

Before his bloodbeards could point out that the creature had abandoned them halfway to Dragonland, he reached for the crown. It was stuck, so he had to brace his good leg against the rock and pull. The crown came free with a sudden jerk, leaving a line of charred blisters across his mother's forehead, and rolled across the cave.

Mordred scrambled after it, picked it up and examined it carefully. Some of the jewels were missing, but it was definitely the same crown his uncle Arthur had worn in their final battle. Triumph filled him. He ran a finger over the dent his axe had made when he'd split the king's helmet from his head, and smiled at the memory.

"Behold the Crown of Dreams!" he announced, showing it to his men. "You see before you one of the four ancient Lights, with more power than Excalibur, and twice as much magic as that useless Lance my cousin stupidly gave to her squire friend! This crown belonged to my uncle Arthur and gave him the power to command men and dragons, and now it's *mine*..." He lifted the glowing circlet above his head.

"Careful, my son!" said his mother in a tone that sent a chill down his spine. "Don't put it on yet."

Mordred scowled as his triumph evaporated. "Why not? I thought that was the whole idea. I've got Pendragon blood, so it won't harm me."

"I've got Pendragon blood too, foolish boy, and it *killed* me."

He lowered the crown and glanced uneasily at his mother's body, which had begun to blacken and shrivel. "How?" he whispered. "How did it kill you?"

"I was careless. There's a jewel missing.

I assumed it was a minor one, knocked out during the battle. But it's one of the magic stones, the one Arthur stored his secrets inside when he sat on the throne of Camelot. You've got to find that jewel and destroy it before the Crown of Dreams will accept you as the next Pendragon."

Mordred looked at the piles of treasure in despair. Find a single jewel among this lot? Worse, what if the stupid dragon had lost the stone on its way here, carrying the crown from the battlefield? It could be lying at the bottom of the Summer Sea.

"We'll be searching all year!"

"No you won't," the witch said. "Because the stone's not lost. If my ex-maid's information is right, it's still at Camelot. Arthur must have taken it out before the battle as a precaution. He left it with Guinevere, and now your cousin has it."

"*Rhianna!*" Mordred clenched his fist in rage. He might have known King Arthur's daughter would stand in his way again. "We have to get it from her," he growled. "I need to raise another army."

"You don't need an army to catch a fly." His mother smiled. "Not even one that stings like your cousin. My ex-maid still has my mirror, so I can control her. This is what we'll do…"

ABOUT THE AUTHOR

Katherine Roberts' muse is a unicorn.
This is what he has to say about her...

My author has lived in King Arthur's country for most of her life. She went to Bath University, where she got a degree in Maths and learned to fly in a glider. Afterwards she worked with racehorses, until she found me in 1984 and wrote her first fantasy story. She won the Branford Boase Award in 2000 with her first book *Song Quest*, and now she has me hard at work on the Pendragon series, searching for the Grail of Stars.

You can find out more about Katherine at www.katherineroberts.co.uk